The Book of Gabriele

A Novel

The Book of Gabriele

A Novel

Richard Cory

Edited by Kathrin DePue

PRESS

ISBN-13: 978-0692182345 (The Press)

ISBN-10: 0692182349

Published in the United States by:

San Francisco | Des Moines | Washington, D.C.

The reimagined is sometimes reality.

Prologue

Starting in 2007, Pope Benedict XVI's butler began stealing secret papal documents. Butler Paolo Gabriele stole the documents to fight what he said was "evil and corruption" in the Holy See. Paolo expressed frustration with a culture of secrecy in the Vatican, which allowed offenses like rape and murder to go unpunished.

"There is a kind of omerta against the truth: not so much because of a power struggle but because of fear and because of caution," Gabriele said in the interview, using the term for the code of silence of the Sicilian Mafia. While he originally reported to acting with "around 20 other people" in the Vatican, he later denied others had been actively involved in helping him.

No one outside of the Catholic Church could have imagined the visible damage that was to follow. And far fewer have any comprehension of what secrets were never released.

This is a story about the destructive power of the mysteries protected by our faith.

Chapter 1

The trunk was dropped at the security desk in the afternoon on a fairly routine day. Michael brought it to the office on a hand cart with the "Up" arrow clearly pointing forward. Michael did not dislike Professor Singh; he just didn't like him enough to run his errands. So if a package didn't arrive on Michael's schedule, he delivered it in whatever manner he saw fit.

If a package was labeled fragile, Michael handled it with care, but this container looked to be a simple, black steamer trunk containing paper documents. During a refurbishment of its storage vaults, the University of Glasgow started digitizing the Hunterian Museum's rare documents. If they were considered valuable to the wider public good, they were shared with Google as part of its digital library initiative. If they crossed Professor Singh's desk, it was because no one else could translate them. But with this nondescript case, there was no indication of how explosive its contents would soon prove to be.

"Morning, Michael," grinned Professor Singh. "How're the ponies?"

Michael invested in a race horse in Belfast a few years back. Even though the money was gone, Michael still vacationed in Belfast to bet on the horses. There was nothing that Michael liked to talk about more than his time at the races. Letting Michael talk about "his ponies" was the easiest way for Raj to get back in Michael's good books.

"Aye, well. Came back Sunday last, a few hundred quid dearer," he said with a twinkle in his eye. In his gruff Govan accent, most of what Michael said sounded like an elongated growl occasionally punctuated by vowels. "You expecting more, or is this it for the day?" Michael said, grumbling again.

"Truth be told, I wasn't expecting this, so I cannae say."

"Hmph. I'll give a ring if there's more," sighed Michael as he slunk back out of the room.

"Iain, let's crack into this when you get a minute," Raj called to the Lecturer in the next room. Iain popped his head in to size up the next load of papers with a wry smile on his face.

"Looks like you were late again, Raj," nodding to the "Up" arrow now pointing down.

"Ech...everyone needs a victory."

***

Ravi was a few years younger than his brother Raj. Where Raj had pursued academia to a point where their father could forgive him for leaving the shop, Ravi had never made it to Raj's level of success. His father could accept Raj leaving the first family grocery on Argyle because he was a world renowned professor who translated ancient texts for MI-6. Ravi, on the other hand, wrote television commercials.

9

Ravi was never in need, and that angered his father the most. He would land a commercial here, another there, making enough to take care of his needs and his beer tab. He did one of the ITV commercials—the one with the frogs. None of his commercials were wildly successful, but they allowed him to sit in coffee shops or pubs all day, paying attention to whatever he fancied. For his father, who went from shop to shop at all times of the day and night, helping Uncle at one, Asher at another, and so on, anytime between seven in the morning and three o'clock the next morning, Ravi's laziness was infuriating.

The fact that Ravi shaved his face and kept his hair short was inexcusable. Where Ravi called it "modernization," his father heard "insult." Ravi was told in no uncertain terms that he should not be seen embarrassing the family on Fridays in the Temple. While he clearly loved his son, he could not have his business partners thinking he could not control his house.

Ravi could see Raj rounding the bowling lawns at Kelvin Way from where he sat at a table by the open window in Mother India Cafe. There was an excited concern on his face—the same one Ravi could hear when Raj called less than an hour ago about meeting at the Cafe.

Raj sat down in a hurry. "We have something big and I need your help," started Raj. Ravi squinted at him. "And I'll pay. I need to get this stuff translated quickly. I think it is something really big."

"How big?"

"This is change the world big," Raj shot back with an excited smile. "If these are what I think, we need to get this right the first time. This will make or break my career." Raj called over for his usual three tapas and Peshwari naan.

"How will this change the world?"

"I think we have a cache of Ali's unpublished writings," beamed Raj. "Do you know what that means?"

"We'll finally find out if he really did get it up Howard Cosell's wife?"

"Aye, Muppet. No, no, no. Ali: as in Islam's first male convert. Muhammad's cousin slash son-in-law turned successor."

"How could you have possibly gotten those?"

"I have no idea," Raj sighed as he leaned back and rested his head in the hammock of his hands. "Michael dropped off a box from Italy some months back, but it didn't come from any of my typical sources and had no identification as to what contract it was for. Assuming it would be clear where it went once we started into it, I had Iain open and process it as if it were any other sensitive delivery. When I finally had time to start getting into it last week, I couldn't believe what I was reading. On one hand, it makes perfect sense. On the other, it is completely unexplainable."

"What does that mean?" Ravi focused his attention on his Karahi as he prepared his jealous little jab. "On one hand you are the only one important enough to receive

11

something like this, and on the other hand you are too important for your time to be wasted by such a trivial discovery? Or how it is that you have so many ragheads in your office but you don't lose your government contracts?"

Raj sat forward as his Saag and Makhni arrived. "Quit being a Muppet—aye, ta, 'ats sound." As the waitress walked away, Raj looked his brother straight in the eye. "I need to work on this with someone I can trust. You always better understood the historical nuances of the language during that time period. I need your help on this. Parts of these documents just make no sense to me. I must be missing something."

In all fairness, Ravi was never mad at Raj. It was just hard to watch Raj get the praise that could have been for him. Ravi made his choices. He walked away from academia on his terms, he was happy with what he was doing, and he was not going to let anyone convince him otherwise. Besides, he was happy. He could do anything he wanted. He could afford to be in the pub by half-ten each morning. What could be better than that, right?

"Like what? What doesn't make sense?" While his interest peaked, he was forcing a nonchalant front by looking out the window at the bowling greens. There was Dr. MacQuay just arriving for an afternoon game with Dr. McKenzie.

"A lot of it looks like shipping details, or invoices. Many are embedded in what looks like personal letters to, who I am thinking right now, must be Abu Talib."

12

"What's wrong with that? Ali basically ran everything for Muhammad. I'd assume he probably organized shipments for his father as well."

"That's fine, but what kinds of things were they into?" Raj leaned in toward Ravi now. It was clear he was about to get into the meat of the project at hand.

"I think he dealt in perfume or something. The Banu Hashim clan was basically responsible for looking after travelers, so trading or supplying gear was probably something Ali would have been involved in," shrugged Ravi.

"Fine, I get the perfume part. If I was seeing Balsam of Mecca or something like that, no bother. But I'm seeing almost none of those types of things mentioned." Raj's wide eyes were looking for some rise to come out of Ravi. "What I'm seeing is opium, and in large quantities."

Ravi cocked his head back, crumpled his mouth to the right, and thought for a minute. "Opium was a pretty widely used medicine back then. The Greeks had their fingerprints all over medical theory at that time, and they loved the opium. I could believe that." Ravi's voice was quickly moving from passive jealousy to intrigued excitement.

"But this is where it gets interesting." It was clear that Raj had been waiting for that slight quiver in his brother's sureness. "In many of these letters, Ali talks about Muhammad taking significant portions of the inventory. He's writing to his father for advice on how to deal with

Muhammad's drug addiction." Raj sat back grinning, as if a lifetime of fame and wealth was now inevitable.

"Sounds like the same pro-Christian garbage that has been circulating for centuries," Ravi snorted. "You're probably just getting duped on this one. You'll be the Muppet headlining the next Dan Brown novel," he said with a sideways grin.

"That's what I waited to tell you. I carbon dated a few samples from some of the original documents that were in the box." Raj paused for effect, hoping the awe of his discovery would soon come back to his brother's face. "They're from the time period. I think there is good reason to believe that these are authentic."

"If that's the one answer you're looking for, it'll be the only answer you'll get, you know." Even if the documents were real, having a clan of merchants selling medical supplies was not revolutionary.

"Well, what about the trafficking of women? It seems like there are whole logs where Ali is buying and selling a wide range of girls, with the same problem: Muhammad is siphoning off product for his own use. Any thoughts on that?"

"My initial thought is that everyone knows mut'ah existed back then. It's pretty clear that the earliest argument regarding whether it was even officially banned didn't occur until after Muhammad died. So of course he had prostitutes."

"But were they selling the women?" Raj retorted. "My understanding is that mut'ah was a very local thing. I've never heard of the buying and selling that it looks like was going on according to these ledgers." With Ravi still unconvinced, Raj threw out his final wildcard "Besides, what else are you doing? Getting paid to prove me wrong is better than paying to drink all day."

That was a pretty valid point. With a shrug of the shoulders, Ravi was in. "Aye, if you're paying, I can find the time to prove you're a Muppet." But as they both turned back to their food, Ravi had one more detail to sort out. "Are you planning on officially contracting me through the Uni? Just make sure the paperwork doesn't bring the fatwa down on me if we do find something here."

Raj had him. Ravi was in, and he knew he had something here. The smile returned to Raj's face as his Achari hit the table. "Don't worry. At the rate Margret processes expenses, fatwas will be as common in Islam as opium and prostitutes by the time you get paid."

***

Raj's office was on the second floor of the East Quadrangle with a gorgeous southeast facing view. Just like many things at the University that ended up in strange places, he got there because no one was paying attention to him. He was originally assigned to his office as one of four researchers within the School of Geographical and Earth Sciences. As his contracts expanded due to the war in Afghanistan, and his coworkers either left or were relocated into the Hetherington Building. No one challenged him for the room. He just stayed, quietly moved his people closer, and built his own corner office kingdom before any unified opposition materialized within the faculty.

The British higher education system was still in the throes of transition. While student fees increased south of the border, Scottish Universities were struggling with their response to reduced budgets and provide greater financial transparency. Professors could no longer just sit in their offices for decades. Aberdeen had brought in an American to "modernize" its strategy, Alumni Associations were forming to continually beg graduates for a greater and greater portion of their wages, and the ever growing yellow-tide of Chinese nationals was the most visible, day-to-day side effect of the Full Cost Accounting approach to higher education. It was also the reason no one was actually able to move Raj from his prized perch. His MI-6 contracts were the most valuable commodity in the entire Main Building and rivaled anything that was going on in the James Watt Nanofabrication Center next door.

It had been years since Ravi visited Raj's office. It was a tornado of tapping keyboards, muffled recordings, and glasses cleaner. The main office door was the exact same wooden door that everyone else had in this section of the building. The reinforced door behind it was not.

The most striking, post-2005 London bombings feature within the office was the suspended secure room. Raj's team dubbed it The Cage. It looked like a short shipping container; The Cage was suspended within a steel frame and had only a single vault door at one end. There were no wires going in or out. All power was brought into The Cage using rechargeable batteries. Vents on each side brought in air from the room, but anyone in The Cage could live on the internal oxygen tanks for up to 48 hours if someone were to launch a biological attack on the premises. As comforting as it would be to know you could live in there that long, Ravi wasn't sure he could work in an environment where the threat of biological warfare was more than just a delusion harbored by the insane.

"Pretty cool gear, eh?" Raj was extremely proud of The Cage. The fact that Raj, a traditional Sikh, had enough clout that MI-6 was willing to fund his own research team in a location of his choosing meant Raj had made it to the top. "Remember back when they rounded us all up after September 11th?" Raj beamed as he stood up to show off The Cage to his brother. "Who would have thought one of us would have gone on to build this in here?"

As Raj pressed his thumb to the pad, looked into the retina scanner, and then entered five sets of alphanumeric codes, Ravi couldn't help but wonder if he should even be allowed to see what was inside the vault-like crate. When the door opened with a slight swoosh of air, he quickly realized it was nothing to get excited about: some basic PCs and an industrial scanner in the middle of a couple hundred hard drives. Ravi looked in, looked back to the outside of The Cage, and back in again. "You must have...three by three by...five...forty-five cubic meters of hard drives in there?"

"I think you know I can't tell you that," Raj said with a grin.

He stepped up into The Cage and in front of a row of drawers. "We start anything unknown off in here, work through it until we know what its protection level should be, and then handle it appropriately from there." He came back with a small drive. "This really good stuff has yet to leave The Cage," he said, gently waving the drive in his hand. "But we have started some semi-public work that is yielding some pretty interesting results."

Raj looked around the other side of The Cage and called to the little man sitting across the room. "Veli, you have time to go over what you have been finding?" He nodded silently, picked up his things, and the three of them headed for the table next to Raj's desk. As they walked, Raj whispered to Ravi, "Veli's a weird little fucker from Albania. He's amazing from an economic forensics point of view: basically at a genius or even savant level. He just can't figure out people. Some French lass in the math department is tormenting him, and he can't figure out that she just wants him to shag her brains out. Would hate to see that collection of smelly, hairy flesh figuring that puzzle out..." Raj went silent as Veli got to within earshot. It was impossible to know what the short troll of a man could hear, though, as the only part of his face he seemed capable of moving at the moment was his eyes.

As they sat down, Veli set up his laptop square with the desk, his paper square to his laptop, and his pen on the paper parallel to the top edge. "Start loading the latest onto here while we talk through what you've found," Raj said. Veli took the drive, silently plugged it in, and after lining it up square with the laptop, started the file transfer. As his laptop whirred away, he put his hands in his lap and waited silently. Raj spoke first. "So, where are we?"

"We are at sixty-five percent confidence on seventy-eight percent of the likely connections. Of these seventy-eight percent, the median number of control paths at the fifty-percent level is three, although the average is eight at this point in time. There are a few low probability paths that I cannot rule out." Veli blinked.

Raj's smile was even wider now and his voice was a mixture of leading investigation and hopeful inquiry. "What is our lowest probability path? Where is al-Qaeda?"

"There are a few south-Asian trucking gangs that traffic rural Indian women between Kolkata and Chennai. I am grouping these individually, but I have not applied this grouping to my summary calculations, which is why there is such a skew. For paths with a high uncertainty, there are a few insurance fraud syndicates in western Canada that are strongly linked to groups out of Hong Kong. These are very uncertain, but the outlier scenarios could show strong direct connection." Second blink.

"What are these linking against? What are you guys meaning by paths?" Ravi looked at the two as if he was on the outside of the funniest inside joke everyone else had already heard. "What is going on between regional sex trafficking and Canadian insurance fraud?"

"The Catholic Church," Raj said quietly. Between Raj's open smile and Veli's open eyes, the two of them were nearly frozen in the picture their numbers created.

"You're surely talking pish," Ravi exclaimed. "You're bloody right this will break your career!"

"There is nothing wrong with these numbers!" Veli snapped from silent to irate, but while his body shook with vengeful anger, his hands remained in his lap and his blinking actually slowed. "Who are you to say my calculations are wrong? I will not work in this environment!"

"Oy, oy, oy…No one is saying that," soothed Raj as he sat forward in his chair in more of an attempt to comfort the shocked Ravi than restrain the volatile Veli. "No one doubts the calculations."

"I will not have my work questioned by the uninformed. The numbers do not lie, and I create the numbers." Veli had not yet taken his eyes off of Ravi. "Al-Qaeda is one-point-eight with an alpha of less than two-percent at the fifty percent level."

So many questions were running through his head, but Ravi wasn't sure whether he wanted to be in The Cage before asking the next one. Thankfully, Raj jumped in first.

"Veli, can you break down what that means for Ravi?"

After a quick half-blink, Veli spoke to Ravi in a tone that sounded like he was reading out of a text book. "The number of paths is the ratio of the number of controlling connections one entity has over another, weighted in a manner to account for dilution, divided by the total number of entities that exert meaningful control. For example, if the path number is unity, it means that every decision made by an organization is directed by the controlling organization. If the path number is thirty-three, it means that only one-third of the decisions occurred at the direction of the controlling entity. We are using the fifty-percent standard, meaning an action is attributed to the controlling entity if the link is more likely than not." Blink five. "Of course, it is important to note, this is only accounting for criminal activity that has a probability of meaningful organization greater than eighty percent. This number includes all known acts that were either claimed by or attributed to the organization with a certainty greater than ninety-five percent. So we may be underestimating the connection."

"Are you implying that over half of all acts committed by al-Qaeda are directed by the Catholic Church?" Ravi looked back and forth between Veli and Raj. Neither of them flinched.

"No. I am saying that over fifty-five percent of the acts committed by al-Qaeda are more than likely performed at the direction of someone within the Catholic Church," Veli replied.

While Ravi's first desired response was, "Bullocks," Veli's previous reaction made that a frightening option and decided to stay quiet. The laptop was now silent. "Veli, I'll just talk to Ravi on my own," Raj said. "Everything is on here now?"

"Yes. Let me disconnect it...from..." In a few clicks it was unplugged and resting detached on the table. "There. I will be over there if you need me." He carefully closed his laptop, placed his blank paper square on top of it, placed his pen on the laptop parallel the paper, and picked it all up as one uniform, static parcel. Raj watched him go, and Ravi's mind fluttered back and forth from Veli's disappearing reflection in the window to the intriguing conclusions Veli presented.

"Where on this earth are you getting enough data to even start making those calculations?" Ravi said when Veli was out of sight.

"Surprisingly, most of it is publicly available." Raj had three computers in his work area. One was connected to the outside world, one was connected to the network in his office, and one was isolated. All of them hooked up to a bank of nine monitors. Across the right three, he brought up window after window of data. "As it is with every project, the key was sent to us. I'm assuming it was the same source as the trunk." As he clicked and scrolled through the windows, shifting some over to other screens, discarding some as if Ravi had seen those before, he spoke to each as he looked at them. "The bulk of the data was lists of bank accounts, lists of telephone numbers, Skype or email aliases, contact sheets, call logs, data packet shipping logs, etcetera. You name it, it was in here. It was like a Rosetta Stone of organized crime."

With another click, Raj pulled up a massive spider web of data points and connections. "Mathematically, we can see how the various contracts flow. This is no different than any other analysis of military, paramilitary, or organized crime organization. We can see data links and money flows. We can see some movements and some meetings. We can see some indications of causation, but some of them are completely counter intuitive." He clicked and zoomed on a jumble of connectors. "For example: this."

They sat in silence for a moment as Raj stared at the screen. It was nothing but a series of letters and numbers, many of them actually in Greek. Before he lost his brother to deeper contemplation, Ravi asked "...and?"

"Aye, aye. Right here, for example, we are seeing patterns of coordination between leaders, or their conduits, in the Muslim Brotherhood and their opposites in the Royal Black Institution." He zoomed back out, scanned for another location, and zoomed in again. "Here we are seeing communication patterns at the C Street House in Washington, DC, that are most similar to places like this: a brothel in a Black Sea resort town that caters to Russian oligarchs."

"C Street House?"

"Don't you remember that one? It was that house full of conservative evangelical politicians?" But American politics were the farthest thing from Ravi's mind. "No bother. Well, the funny thing about the Black Sea brothels, as you see here, is that they have a communication pattern into the Eastern Orthodox Church, not the other way around." He sat and stared at the screens for a bit longer, not moving anything. His mind was clearly elsewhere. "Very odd..."

"You are sure the model can't be off?" Ravi was far from a mathematical genius, but he knew history. Unexpected correlations will always exist in the world, but at their heart is a causation that was once logical.

As if he was reading Ravi's mind, Raj stopped what he was doing and looked straight at him. "The data is accurate. It's informative. But we can't explain it. That is where I need you."

"Where do you think I should start?"

"Well, this is where it could be fun." Raj pulled a binder from the other side of his desk and put it in front of Ravi. "The chattiest groups are in South America. Drug cartels. When looking at their activities as a whole, the Catholic Church has a pretty high path value." Ravi's crumpled brow forced Raj to stop and take a quick detour. "Sorry, I mean they were getting most of their orders internally. But when we started to look at their highest value activities--things like gun running, major shipments, murders—the path value started to approach unity quickly." Raj pointed to the drive still sitting in perfect line with the desk's edge. "That is everything we know right now. Do not hook it up to the internet and do not connect it to a public computer. Take that laptop there. It is fully clean. All of this work I have here, you have there."

Ravi started looking through the binder, page after page of broken Spanish fragments. "And this?"

"Those are the communiques that we cannot figure out. We think we decrypted them correctly, but none of them really make a whole lot of sense. We are not sure if it is a dialect thing, like maybe they are mixing fragments of Brazilian Portuguese into the language, or something else. It may be that our equations arrived at garbage, or it may be that it is something like that old American trick with the Navajos in the Pacific during World War Two. We need someone good to go through it." He was looking at Ravi as if he was hoping Ravi would read between the lines.

"So, since you know Romanic languages are not my area or specialty, what did you have in mind?"

With a pair of eyebrow raises, he grinned back, "Well, I thought maybe you and Sophia could work this one out?"

"Are you taking the fucking piss?"

"Brov, things change. She's not in my group anymore, but she's still phenomenal at this type of work."

"So ask her yourself, you twat." Raj had set up Ravi and Sophia for the first time years ago. Raj also wrote the contract that put Sophia on a research team with Gavin, which turned into more than merely academic discoveries.

"Brov, you need this job, and to get this part of the job done, you need Sophia's help."

Ravi sank back and stared at his brother for a moment, taking it all in. Somehow, the implausibility of uncovering some of the most fundamentally implausible criminal relationships had just been trumped by the suggestion that Ravi confront an old girlfriend. "What room is she in now?"

"Just five doors down. You'll find your way home," Raj said with a grin. As Ravi sat forward to collect himself, Raj settled back into his chair as if he was in the pretext to a deep contemplation.

"You know, the most curious part of these traditional crime syndicates is the power structure. We had always looked at these cartels like competitors attempting to gain market share." Raj grabbed the end of his nose, pressed his nostrils closed and released them at random, as if attempting to kick-start his brain. "But there really seems to be two parts; it's almost like they have essentially parallel leadership. They seem to operate like predestined entities that have only been given partial free will by a sovereign being of some kind. Even when separate cartels are stable and predictable, the whole market remains tumultuous. Where one area, like gun violence, goes down, another, like the drug trafficking, goes up. All the while, there seems to be some kind of order to the violence; no single entity ever gets all the control. There is always a kind of higher balance, giving and taking away..."

"Should I file that under philosophy, or leads that everyone already knew?" When Ravi's smirk was not returned, he began to sense that the joke was on him.

"The pattern indicated by our numbers continues to rise no matter what is happening in this part of the world. And it's not a new pattern either." Ravi had no quick response to his brother's ruminations and could do nothing but shake his head. In a half-whisper, half-shudder, with a stare that seemed like it could break Ravi in half, Raj said, "The criminal market share...controlled by the Pope."

Chapter 2

"Well, well, well...Ribbit, ribbit, Tadpole."

"Lovely to see you, too, Sophia." As Ravi's grin met her inviting eyes, it felt as if they had last seen each other that morning. "It's been ages," he said as he sat on the edge of her desk and drew in for a one-armed hug.

"To what do I owe the pleasure of your presence?" She slowly turned from one side to the other in her desk chair.

"Should I need a reason to visit a woman so beautiful?"

"I just know it was a bit heated the last time you walked out." She said looking through her eyebrows at him.

"So how is Gavin?"

"He's probably fine." And there it was. "Jennifer would know better."

"Your old mate Jennifer?"

She nodded and rolled her eyes. "They seemed to have a similar drinking schedule," she commented as she sat down. "Came back from a conference and found out they had taken up the same sleeping schedule as well." Her head twitched to the side, as if it were a typewriter shaking off the last line. Her grin was again trained on Ravi. "What can I do for you?"

"Well, with that bloke gone...Plenty," he flirted back. "I might need your hands," he grinned playfully.

"And where do you need those?"

"Working through these documents." He set down the binder without breaking her gaze. It was odd to him how he could act so bold when he was so crushed when he found out she was cheating. He couldn't trust her with his heart, but he was becoming more and more certain that giving her this binder meant he was about to trust her with Raj's life and his own.

"What are they?" She pulled her glasses over her nose from where they hung at her open, V-necked collar and started to flip through the pages.

"We think they are decrypted communications between warlords and South American drug cartels. We just aren't sure what they mean." Bringing back the charm, he said, "As you know, romance not my specialty."

"Well, that sounds like fun. So what are they really?"

Ravi didn't flinch, and her smile faded. He waited as her face went from playful to concern and settled on determined. "Raj needs you on this. And I need your discretion. I'm trusting you with something big here."

She held his stare for another moment before turning her attention to the binder.

"It looks like new world Spanish with various slang mixed in. Shouldn't take me too long to translate. What do you need and by when?"

"I need you to read through this here and then talk it through with me. I want to be sure I understand what is written here entirely."

"No problem. I don't have class for a few hours." With the smile back to her face she said, "And I'd be happy to drop everything for you."

"If only that were necessary, Love," he shot back as he stood and backed away from her toward the door. "Just ring me when you're ready to talk through them." As he grabbed the door handle, he paused for a quick moment and she looked at him. "This needs to stay under the hat for now."

"No problem. I'll see you as soon as I get through what's here."

***

Ravi always liked exiting the Main Building at the Memorial Gates. Those names on the gates—from Watt to Cullen, Adam Smith to Lister—were inspiring. He paused as he reached them, staring through the golden letters and paying homage to the more than half a millennia of history at the University. It was hard to shake his disappointment as he looked at them today; where the gates once inspired him, they now revived the painful memory of his failures. They named greatness, and he was not on the list. He looked down at the ground with a sigh before continuing up to University Gardens.

As he walked in the door, Anne just happened to be sitting in the vestibule. "Ravi?" She got up, stood in that awkward position between strained hug and hand shake, and they ended up patting each other on the upper arm. "How nice to see you. What have you been up to?"

"Just continuing to write. Commercials, actually."

"Really? You always were a great writer," Anne's face always showed her thoughts, and she was clearly confused. "Commercials? Like what kinds of commercials?"

"Just regular commercials on the tele. I did the ITV commercial with the frogs, you know it?"

"I think so." She cocked her head as if watching the commercial in her mind. "But there isn't any talking in it, is there? Isn't it just the frogs and the announcer?"

"Aye, that's the one. It's my favorite example. Ironic, really," he said with a smile.

"Hmmm. Ok," she seemed happy enough to remain confused and move on. "Are you here to see anyone in particular?"

"Just hoping to chat with Dave for a little bit. Is he around?"

"I think he's in a lecture for a while yet. I'm sure it would be no problem if you wanted to wait in the library for him. We'd be happy to have you in the building again," she said with a smile. "Maybe you can do your next commercial on the mice we keep finding in there? I'm not sure they would do much speaking either."

Ravi gave a humored snort. "It does make the dialogue easier," he joked. "It's great to see you. I'll just be down the hall, then."

The library was essentially an oversized lounge for the history department. It used to hold one copy of every PhD thesis written within the department, but now it was only home to those of notable distinction; the rest were housed in the Macintosh library next door. While capable of tightly fitting all of the Faculty and Staff for important announcements or meetings, it remained mostly empty for the bulk of the day except for those who would occasionally take their tea there. Ravi sat down on the couch and opened the drive with his brother's laptop.

The drive was massive and nearly full with almost fifty terabytes of data. All of the data had been meticulously catalogued, and most of it had been translated with annotations. All of it was organized using the spider map of relationships.

With every layer that he began clicking through, the connections became more unbelievable: Weapons sales were originating with Israeli officials and transferred through Hasidic clerics to Egyptians before arriving in the hands of Hamas. Columbian drugs were being delivered through American churches for street distribution in the Church communities. Prostitutes were being trafficked through Eastern Europe to Western think tanks—the brothels of political leadership—and pressed into service across the world. And in every transaction, Rome was at the center of each deal. It had to be wrong.

David walked into the room with large, lanky steps. Ravi started to get up before being shooed down, as David twisted himself onto the couch, crossing and folding his appendages. "Haven't seen you in a while," he grinned. "To what do I owe the honor?"

"Well, prozzies, actually," Ravi's grin was returned as both recalled how they used to take the long route back to the West End from a night out along Argyle.

"We are all little more than prostitutes for this fine institution," remarked David. "So I am afraid you will have to be a bit more specific."

"Funny you should mention prostitutes: I need to know a bit more about mut'ah. I've always known it to basically be the origin of prostitution, polygamy and harems in the eastern world," David's eyes started narrowing in expectation of the question. "My understanding is that these were all local girls who were basically passed around the tribe. Was there more to it?"

"Well, there are the clear parts and then there are the not so clear parts," David began. David's head slowly bobbled as he retrieved various pieces of data from the different physical locations that made up his memory. "We know this came into being because Muhammad couldn't stop shagging women he shouldn't have been shagging. Like any great leader, depending on how you define greatness, he was prolific. This part is pretty well known." He began to uncoil himself and walk to one of the walls. "Don't get up, I'm coming right back as soon as I find...ah, this one here." His voice trailed off into the pages of a medium-sized doctoral thesis.

"This is a very interesting piece of work that looks at mut'ah as Muhammad practiced it, so to speak. The candidate spent over a decade painstakingly piecing together the likely sources of all the women Muhammad was shagging and heat mapped those locations," and after flipping through a few more pages, David handed the text over to Ravi. "But he then started to heat map where they and their descendants went after he got rid of them." Ravi started to slowly turn the pages, watching two graphs per page expand and crawl across the world.

"The two graphs were plotted with two different reference points. The candidate used the same delta-t from both references on a single page, so they are a little confusing. There is no way to truly line them up in a meaningful way, so you can't really draw the kinds of inferences you would expect from each of the two graphs on the same page." David pursed his lips and shook his head as if the student was right there in front of him. "I asked him not to be so daft, but aspiring academics are worse than the object of their fascination."

"And the two reference points?"

"Oh, yes. Sorry," he coiled back into a tangled mess on the couch and continued. "The top plot on each page uses his exile as the t-zero event. The bottom plot sets t-zero as the death of Abu Talib," David craned his head as Ravi flipped, attempting to help him make sense of the images. "They're a little confusing, which was always the problem with this thesis. It was never really clear what it all meant. I wasn't convinced at the time that these were very appropriate reference dates as it didn't make a whole lot of sense to me. I wasn't convinced that these subtle variations were of any interest."

As David lost himself in the pages, it was clear to Ravi that he was missing something.

"Oy, Muppet, can you hurry up and tell me what we're looking at?"

"Superficially, we're looking at an individual whose conquests started off relatively local before they began traveling farther and farther to get to him and farther yet after he had shagged them. So we found out, a little too late, that we were, fundamentally, looking at a sex trafficker."

Ravi saw that the maps spread deeper into Europe over time. If Muhammad was a trafficker, it made sense to watch the maps grow from east to west throughout the Roman Empire. The more interesting part was the series of lulls in growth. For periods of time the map changed very little before taking off again.

"Come back to my office. The next piece of work should connect a few more dots," he said as he stood up. Ravi was still engrossed in the colors on the maps as they grew like a tumor infecting the region while he followed David down the hall.

"Wow, you've moved up," Ravi said when he looked up from the page at David's office. The window had a gorgeous view of the main building to the south and a view down past the Queen Margaret Union towards Byres Road to the west.

"You'd be sitting here if you would have stayed," David shrugged. "But, I can see the appeal of writing dialogue-free commercials."

As he sat in front of his computer screen, he clicked through the string of file folders and they expanded in a series as if each click was the next element of a secret code. As the appropriate Word file loaded, David started to explain the premise behind what they were about to see. "The original work was really done to show that Muhammad was a hypocrite and that mut'ah was just an excuse to do what he wanted. While it essentially gave colorful images to reinforce that understanding, it also started to look at the associations of these sex slaves in a more general sense both before and after Muhammad was involved."

As he clicked through the various charts and images, he slowly shook his head. "It was all such a shame. This was such great work."

"What was a shame?"

"The young woman who was working on this was assaulted by a pack of neds outside her apartment in New Maryhill. They cut her a smile, gang raped her, and left her to die. And just to make sure, they burned her house to the ground. Her lungs were full of smoke. I can't think of a more terrifying way to go." He was motionless for a moment as his head was stuck on the image of those events that he could only ever imagine. "We had just selected her external reviewer. It never went any farther. This is the only summary of the work. The only reference materials she had control of were in her house."

"Are you fucking kidding? A pack of neds did that?" David remained transfixed on the screen.

"Police seemed certain. They found the kids, prosecuted them." He repeated the facts as dryly as they existed. Empty and hollow. "You could go speak with them, if you can find them."

Softly and quietly, Ravi attempted to bring the conversation back out of that house. "What did she find?"

After a brief moment, the question jolted David out of that fire, that house, his colleague battered on the floor, and her mangled flesh being eaten by the flames. "In short, she asserted that there is a pattern of where these women came from and started to go to. She concluded that the Banu Hashim clan had been actively trafficking women from all over the region and North Africa in no particular pattern. It was a basic sex trade that accompanied their better known perfume sales. But, at a certain point right around when Muhammad had his visions in the cave, the origin of these women began to localize around Palestine, while their traffic pattern becomes more targeted. In essence, there was a strain of women that were being delivered more broadly in a geographical sense, but only to influential leaders of tribes, countries, and after Muhammad is gone, to clergy throughout Europe. It is fascinating."

"They were basically becoming a procurement service for the elite?"

"Procurement service would imply that the shippers were mere servants. We can't be sure of that," David mused as he stared at the writings before him on the screen. "Sometime in the mid to late six hundreds, the supply lines become less clear. That could have been a whole other line of study to look into how this niche network essentially fell apart. Like many of these things, it just faded. Who knows?" He spun around in his chair, slapped his hands against his knees, and addressed Ravi. "So, that get us anywhere on your question about mut'ah?"

"Aye, give me plenty to consider." Ravi sat there for a moment contemplating whether it was the right call to come to David for help, but he ended up believing he could trust David. "Have you spoken to my brother recently?"

"Not really. I see him over at the University Club from time to time, but that's it. Why?"

"He has a trove of information now that could probably help you find some more answers. You should call in on him sometime."

"Can you elaborate at all, or is this one of his secret projects he's not supposed to be on anyway?" David grinned. Raj was the closest thing to a spook currently operating at the University.

"I really don't know what I can say. Just ring him; the extension should be three-four-one-one."

"Okay. I will as soon as I can."

"Well, I'll let you get to it then," Ravi said as he stood up.

"Are you working at all right now?"

"Not really. I'm just considering a few things." He flashed David a grin and pointed at him as he turned to go. "You need to call Raj. It'll be right up your alley."

***

As Ravi entered the quadrangle from the cloisters, he saw Michael exchanging solemn pleasantries with a dark figure. There was something unforgettably captivating about Michael. He was clearly old but even more weathered than his years. Ravi attempted to peek at the man Michael spoke to from across the grass where he moved away along a different sidewalk path. Just as Ravi was about to look away from the strange figure for the last time, the man's eyes forced him to engage. There was a purposeful hollowness to them that froze Ravi's heart and rooted Ravi's feet to the ground where he stopped. The man finally looked away and disappeared around the gate. Ravi turned to continue walking and almost tripped over Michael who suddenly appeared in front of him.

"You'll be meeting your brother at the Tap."

There was something startlingly calm but clearly agitated in Michael's voice. "What?"

"You will take your tea at the Tap. I'm not asking you." Michael's eyes slowly darted between Ravi, the ground, the cloisters, and the absence of the man. As his eyes shifted, his gaze drifted off to another time and place. "I've seen too much and done too little many a'time." He shifted his jacket collar enough to reveal an Orange Order pin. "You and your brother have always kept me as kin. I dinnae ken how you got into this. I'd never want the Royal Blacks taking any mind of me. I just hope you make it out."

Ravi held his eyes for a moment. "Michael..."

"I dinnae ken what you know, and I dinnae ken what you don't. I know you need to be taking your tea at the Tap." He turned and faded into the greyness of the unlit corridor. As Michael left, Ravi sat at the doorway for a moment. He knew he should heed Michael's advice, but he wasn't sure if he should visit the office first. He pulled his cellphone out, texted Raj about meeting at the pub, and paused for a response. He looked up and around, hoping to see something: hoping to see answers to explain this strange confrontation.

Glancing at his silent phone one last time, he turned and walked into the balmy day. The Tap was directly ahead of him. He enjoyed watching football there because it looked straight back at the University through the bowling and croquet lawns. When he got bored watching football, he would turn from the televisions and drink to the life at the University he had given up. It was always easier to pin his desperation on a collection of buildings than on the person or the past to which it belonged.

"Aye, lager," he nodded to the barman before texting Raj again. The Tap was always empty in the afternoon, save the joiners who started arriving around three in the afternoon and remained there until their daily wages were spent. The food was awful so no one came for lunch or a late afternoon snack. Ravi sat down at his usual table and looked toward his brother's dark office windows. Where could he be?

Marnie grabbed the pint from the barman, put it down for Ravi and sat down herself with a grin. "Fancy a wager on tomorrow's Old Firm match?" Ravi's father made the conscious choice of aggressively raising his family as Partick Thistle fans for the sole purpose of avoiding the rivalry's sectarianism. He took the boys to every match he could, just so he could make sure all of their earliest sporting memories were attached to Firhill. He let them play rugby because he didn't see any of the sectarianism there, and he thought it was a great way for his sons to be respected as members of the upper-middle class. Ravi gave up on rugby when he got through school, but he kept his Thistle alliance.

"Aye. Your boys will get buggered," he said with a half-smirk. He went back to his drink, unable to smile through his nerves. Michael had never revealed allegiances, he never offered meaningful advice to any of the Faculty, and he never looked scared. Ravi's meeting with him in the quad had Ravi shook. Ravi texted Raj again. Where the fuck are you?

"What's the matter, Chinkie?" She knew that sarcastic term of endearment always made him smile. After all, he was the only person she knew who could tell Japanese from Chinese or Vietnamese from every other Asian ethnicity. All that she got from him today was a reluctant grin.

"Just worried about..." As he began to speak, he saw his brother's office light turn on. "Ech, give me a second..." He hit the call button and put the phone to his ear as it started to ring.

"Oy, just got your texts. Are you at the Tap?"

"Aye. Did you see Michael?"

"No, why?"

"He said we needed to grab tea. I was expecting to find you here."

"What? No, I've been in a tutorial for the past hour and..." His voice trailed off as something distracted him. "Uh... give me a second here."

"Why? What's going on?"

"It looks like Michael must have just dropped off...uh, just dropped off a few new trunks...I'm just trying to..."

The initial spark was so unexpected that the flames had nearly rolled completely out of the windows before Ravi could even recognize what had happened. While physically impossible, he could almost feel the heat before the pressure waves arrived. He knew Marnie was screaming on the floor, he knew the barman was already lunging for a phone to call the police, and he knew he would soon feel something.

But, for the moment, he was numb.

Chapter 3

The greatest challenge in organizing the Antam Sanskar was the debate between Ravi's mother and the Guru over where in the process each ceremony should start. His mother argued that since her son had essentially vaporized in a fire, reciting the Shabads would be offensive. This was her way of denying what had happened. It was her way of denying that her son had finally returned to God. It was her way of avoiding the family and friends who would be expecting to see her quiet, strong, and reverent. She felt she had been in Britain too long and feared her faith was not strong enough to successfully weather this test. Raj was her favorite son. No matter what she was told to believe, no matter how much she believed before he was born that she would only be a temporary caregiver for the vessel that momentarily contained his soul, her son was dead, and she was unable to reconcile her beliefs with her grief.

Raj had worked in a world that was so foreign to his family and the world of his kin, that the guests barely knew the man they had come to pay respects to. Only a few of his family and friends knew anything of his work; most of them had never met any of his colleagues, and only an isolated minority had ever even known which part of the University housed his office. Ravi made it through the ceremony just like their mother: by pretending it was not happening. In less than ninety minutes total, all sacred duties were done, and Raj was in heaven, awaiting a new body to bring him back to Earth.

One hundred, seventy-four missed calls and four hundred, forty-six text messages later, hiding from the daylight in his Partick apartment, Ravi finally got up to answer a knock at the door. He was part expecting, part hoping, and part dreading the fact that is was Sophia. It had been before, and it would have been again if he didn't eventually answer. Her face bore a red mixture of grief and terror; it was clear that she had not slept for days. She looked like she had been searching for something—or someone—that could make her feel safe again. She looked up at Ravi through swollen, strained eyes, as if pleading with him to protect her—if he could.

She fell in the door as soon as soon as Ravi opened it wide enough. Ravi stood solid like a cement pillar with arms as she buried her sobs in his chest. They stood there for several minutes before walking into the apartment and closing the door tight behind them.

They fell on the couch where they stayed for almost a full twenty four hours in silence. They both fell in and out of consciousness: switching between what were and what they hoped were dreams. Once her tears had run dry and Ravi could muster the will to speak, he asked her if she had been home since Raj's funeral.

"Yes, the Police have been sitting outside for the past two weeks," she said. "The squad car is gone, but they tell me there is one detective who will be watching my flat for a while. They say they are monitoring all major research partners Raj recently had."

"Wasn't your last contract with him done years ago now?"

She flinched and went silent again.

"We're going to need to get this in the open," he urged.

"I never stopped working with Raj," she spoke loud, but it sounded like an apology. "I have been rebuilding the CIA's wars in central and South America from one angle, and he was continually building them from another. We had to keep working together."

"So when I brought you these fragments, you already knew all about them?"

"I wasn't on the same page with those. I'm still not completely clear what project those were for," she said defensively. "They don't fit any of the other contracts we are working on."

"They weren't on any contract. It was just some side job Raj had come across. That is where I was supposed to start getting involved." He sat there looking at the cushion he was sitting on before leaning his head back against the sofa to stare at the ceiling. "So what do the fragments say?"

"The translations don't make a whole lot of sense to me. The fragments seem to be a series of jumbled negotiations. If you read them at face value, it sounds like each Catholic diocese was negotiating and managing part of the drug trade. At the same time, the local parishes were negotiating money for everything from rehab to rebuilding funds. And many of these conversations made it seem as though funds came from the drug runners. It didn't make any sense."

"What do you mean the dioceses were negotiating and managing drug trades?"

"I mean just that. They were tracking shipments, planning who would get how much and when, and defining everyone's share of the profits," she said, sitting up straight now. "The oddest part of each conversation is that the dioceses were defining the volume of each shipment. They said how much would be available with each shipment. It almost seems like the drug cartels were answering to their local diocese. It doesn't make any sense."

"Suppose it makes sense if you believe the Catholic Church is managing the drug trade."

Sophia snorted and grinned sarcastically. "Right, the Pope is controlling drug gangs. That makes a lot of sense."

"So does my brother getting blown up by the janitor," Ravi retorted. He knew the comment would cut deep. Too deep. He was ashamed to have said it the moment it passed his lips.

Sophia's smile vanished as the comment brought her from contemplation right back to terror. "Ravi, a fatwa on any of us was only a matter of time. Our work has led to more targeted killings, more drone strikes, and more renditions than any MI-6 operation. What they see on the ground is only a fraction of what we find for them." She gazed over Ravi's head as if focusing on some far off battle field. "Raj sat each of us down when we first started and clearly outlined the risks. None of us really comprehended what he was saying until we were in too deep: until we could no longer leave. He would remind us from time to time that we had discussed what was happening and that we were taking precautions for this. But no one really takes the right precautions; no one takes enough precautions. We didn't really think we needed to. We aren't soldiers. We are just working in the academic world. None of us fully understood that our work killed people."

She sat for a moment curling her knees closer to her chest. In a quiet voice, she nearly whispered, "And now it has killed one of our own. No one can ever prepare for that."

***

Another full day passed in silence before Ravi started to look through his missed call log. Many calls were from Sophia, but most were from his mother and father. A few were from colleagues that knew Ravi and Raj. David McKenzie had called three times. He rang the number back and hung up when it went straight to voicemail. A few numbers were not in his contacts log: mostly mobile phone numbers, a few zero-one-four-one numbers. But one number caught his eye: a reporter from ITV that he had only met in passing a few years back. Angus had called over ten times in the past two days.

Ravi searched for any texts from him and found only random fragments. Grab a pint? Or other random questions like: working much lately? None of them said anything about why Angus wanted to talk to Ravi now, and Angus never left a voicemail. Ravi texted him back. The response was immediate.

Òran Mór in five?

Ravi stared for a moment, shot back a 'ya,' and went to this room to change his shirt for the first time in two weeks. He ran out the door, hailed a cab, and arrived in the evening mist outside of the converted church that was now Òran Mór. It looked like Angus had been there for fifteen minutes and one pint. Ravi sat down at least one behind.

Angus wasted no time: "Who else knows what you guys were piecing together?" He looked away long enough to order another pint of the same and then devoted his attention back to Ravi. His voice was clearly worried, but it was unclear whose safety was of concern.

"I'm not sure what you mean? I don't even know what we were piecing together."

"So, you just happen to have a brother who gets blown up, an ex-girlfriend who you just start seeing again that also happens to work on extensive MI-6 contracts, and you just started to reconnect with a professor that is now in a coma? Either you are the cause, or they are all extremely unlucky." He downed nearly half of his second pint.

"What? Who is in a coma?"

"Professor McKenzie went into a coma at Great Western Hospital over a week ago. If you ask me, the prognosis is whatever they want it to be." He polished off pint number two and motioned for another.

"What are you talking about? Who are they?"

Angus stared at Ravi for a second but seemed to read his entire history. "For fuck sake, do you really not know what you are stirring up here?" The blank look on Ravi's face said it all, and Angus buried his face in his hands before peering over the tips of his fingers. "You fucking Muppets. This is fucking rich. You don't even know what you've found." Angus took a quick look around the bar. "We need to talk downstairs." He got up, put enough cash on the bar for eight pints, and led Ravi outside.

Òran Mór had been a church on the corner of Byres Road and Great Western Road before converting into a trendy pub above ground and a night club below. By this point of the evening, a line was already forming, and the music seeped out every time the doormen let another group in. Angus walked up with Ravi behind and was ushered straight in. He glanced at the bar and continued walking through the dance floor to the booths left of the DJ stand. Because of how the speakers were facing, a wall of the latest house music made everything outside of the booths inaudible. In the booth, they could talk with the same ease as they did in the pub upstairs. It became clear why this was Angus's favorite spot to take a confidential source.

Within moments, a bottle service of Smirnoff vodka was brought to the table by a fit, young girl in a mini-kilt. Ravi sat a bit dumbfounded as she poured Angus a glass of vodka with a splash of lemonade and then looked to Ravi. Angus pointed at the table in front of Ravi and she poured Ravi a normal measure, before leaving the table with a wink. She was a very standard Scottish beauty. Her ass was flatter than the state of Iowa, but you could tell that her breasts were deceptively large. It was a Canadian friend who first pointed out this physical anomaly to Ravi. For some reason, no matter how small they looked in clothes, Scottish breasts were almost always happily larger than expected.

Angus watched her leave before speaking again. "I joined the Royal Black Institution taking the same gamble they took on me. The history of those in my position is clear, but men like me turn into little more than reporters or politicians. We never see that our downfall is predestined. We always think we will rise above it. We always assume that we are immune." He quickly finished the first glass of vodka and was already pouring himself another with a smaller splash of lemonade.

"What on—"

"Shut the fuck up. Meeting with you may have been a mistake. Just shut the fuck up while I think this through." He started to sip this next drink and looked out at the dance floor as it filled with more undulating young students followed by young professionals who were hoping to relive the days before their life was predestined at someone else's beck and call. Ravi watched Angus' face, which, like any good poker player's, remained hard as granite while his eyes did all the work. With one more large drink, he set the cup down and fell back into the booth, apparently defeated by the unsuitable options he had come up with.

"You always were the dumbest genius I'd ever met. You fucking cunt. You've right fucked me now." As he leaned his head to the side and looked Ravi straight in the eye, a smile came across his face. "How the fuck did you get them to pay you for a bunch of frogs croaking? You didn't write one actual word?" It was the kind of disarming comment that made them both laugh, and relax for the moment.

"To be fair, 'croak' is still a word, and I did use it a lot." In truth, it was Ravi's favorite television commercial. It was his way of telling all of those cunts to fuck off. He had been getting copy after copy rejected by editors that were too stupid to know what they were reading. They always wanted something flashier, something, "More American." They never knew what exactly it was that they wanted, but it wasn't what some raghead academic was going to give them: until the frogs. It was so ridiculous. He walked in with a page of the word croak written out as if it were a random pattern, each attributed to frog-one through frog-six, and the whole meeting immediately got into a debate of how many croaks Ravi thought could really be expected for each frog. Within moments they were debating whether frog-three could really be expected to offer three or four croaks. The artwork came back, and frogs five and six were cut, which pleased the finance people. Within weeks, Ravi was filming frogs in a box against a black backdrop. It was the most ridiculous exercise he could have imagined, and it forever defined his career. Television viewers didn't get it, advertisers thought it was genius, and the rest were skeptics. Angus was a skeptic.

"You were always such a silly cunt," Angus shook his head as he looked at his drink and then back at Ravi. "I did a whole workup on you. I didn't understand you, so I went back to figure out what the fuck some kid with this much talent was doing in that office. Turns out all the facts said you were a fuck-up: some kid who couldn't get his shit together, didn't get a promotion he wanted, and quit." His voice trailed off as he picked up his drink, thought about it, and offered a final thought before finishing the glass. "Suppose I should have just left it at that."

Angus snorted and poured himself another, halving the amount of lemonade used to dilute his access to bliss.

"Here's the meat of it, as I understand it. The Royal Black Institution makes its money running guns. But running is the operative word. They aren't calling the shots. They do little more than enable the violence that the Orange Order foot soldiers incite and implement."

"How do you know this?" Ravi had yet to touch his own drink, but Angus was pouring yet another without losing a beat. He threw it down like water.

"Because they seek out people like me: reporters or moles who continually gather information. Just like that Russian FBI spy did in America, constantly looking himself up in their system to see if they were onto him, they want people who are scared of them without really knowing why. They gave me complete access to their procedures in the hopes that, once I knew it all, my faith would help me to accept it as just."

Ravi finally scooped up his drink and felt it burn his throat on the way down. He had lost count of how many drinks he had fallen behind, but Angus seemed to still be as clear-headed as before he finished the first pint in the bar upstairs.

"I was hoping that you were in a position to blow the lid off of this shit," Angus said. "I thought if I gave you a missing key or two, you'd already have the rest of the dots to connect it all and help me figure out how deep this shit really went and how goddamn screwed I really am."

As he raised his glass to his mouth, he calmly said "Don't move" before putting his hand in Ravi's pocket. "This is a USB drive that will give you the rest of the evidence you need as long as you have the information I assume you already have. Every file has a virus in it that will seek out a security key that it expects to be embedded on your computer. If your computer connects to the internet, it will be immediately validate any code it finds. If it does not validate the code immediately, or one does not exist on your computer, it will kill your computer within forty-eight hours. If you send the electronic file, you will also be sending the virus. In short, do not put this onto a computer that is attached to the internet, and do not connect this drive anywhere unless you are immediately prepared to use it."

"And printing won't do it?"

"Have you really not figured out how big this is?" Angus sounded worried for the first time in their conversation. "Is that a serious question? Are you really that fucking stupid? This isn't some little country-on-country espionage thing here. Once you connect this to an unapproved computer, it will start a chain of events that are irreversible. You aren't a fucking idiot. How many data sources did your brother have to work with? Where did he get them all from?"

Ravi sat there dumb struck. In all honesty, he had never really thought to ask.

"We are now creating more data than we know what to do with, and that data is seeping out at the seams of every device we are using, from computers, to printers, to telephones. With the right level of interest, people like your brother can capture more data than the average person even knows exist. Fucking listen: do not hook up this thing to anything until you are ready."

The dance floor was now full of girls dancing in circles while guys watched from the sides planning their attack. Each was drinking up the courage to confront the other. Ravi thought about the Scottish waitress for a moment to break away from the tension sitting across from him; the Scottish woman is an interesting beast. They are always looking for a man that is strong enough to tell them what to do, but never a man who expects them to do it. They rule their house, but don't want to lead their household. They are scared of failure, but never consider it. Once you are in the thick of it, they'll cut you quicker than any man. It was a funny reality of the whole nation: old friends can be confused for enemies, and calm environments can mask unexpected fissures. Nothing, it seems, is done in moderation. All is either still or excessive, and it takes a certain type of person to live a life of such volatility.

"You need to get smart real quick here," Angus said, forcing Ravi's attention back to the booth where he sat in terror. "The Orange Order gets its orders form the Royal

Black Institution. The Royal Black Institution sells weapons, so the Orange Order creates conflict that necessitates weapons. The Royal Black Institution gets those guns through the Vatican...I shouldn't have to tell you who is calling the shots around here."

They sat in silence again and watched the dance floor for a while before Ravi mustered up the courage to speak. "So; talking to me: What does that mean for you?"

"One week, tops." The words rolled off his tongue easier than the vodka slid down it. "They don't know what to think of you, yet. I was hoping you knew more than it appears you do. That may save your professor friend."

"What do you mean?"

"He got put under when they saw he had pulled up that unpublished thesis on Muhammad's whores." He stared at the now empty glass, considered another, and like magic, the waitress with the deceptive top was back, bottle in hand. "Another on order?"

"Sure, I'm up," was all Ravi could muster.

"It looks like I called you too early," Angus lamented as she poured his first drink from the new bottle. "I assumed you had already put the other pieces together. I don't know exactly what they are, what they mean, or how to expose the people responsible. But if the Catholic Church is calling the shots for the Orange Order, something is fucked beyond belief."

Surprisingly, those were the clearest words of the night: Muhammad was dealing in whores, the Orange Order is an arm of the Catholic Church, and that means the drug cartels in Central America are controlled by the Pope. It didn't make any rational sense; but then again, nothing in the past few weeks could be explained. They sat in silence, watching the young girls wiggle back and forth like seaweed caught in the tide. For a moment, they both seemed to silently acknowledge this moment as the end of the line. These were the final moments, in a world so beyond explanation, where they were able to see behind the cloak, knowing that their limited knowledge was all they would get. Realizing now that this was the beginning of the end, Ravi longed only for the bliss that writhed there on the dance floor: the kind of bliss that only comes with true ignorance.

***

When Ravi returned, Sophia was awake and sitting at the kitchen table, pouring over a spider map that had started on one page before more and more pieces of paper were required to cover its extent. "It seems to be an amazing network."

"Why is that?" He started to take off his coat, but decided to keep it on for a bit. The weather was starting to turn, and there is nothing that rips through clothes like the wind in western Scotland. Ravi turned the radiator up a little bit more before coming to look over Sophia's shoulder.

"Thank you, it was starting to get cool in here, but I wasn't sure anymore how you liked it." Looking over her shoulder, Ravi attempted to make sense of her handwritten notes as she explained. "The hard lines are ones I know for sure, ones where the fragments are either conclusive or where there doesn't seem to be a reasonable alternative. The dashed lines are ones that are suggested, but the messages could be interpreted another way. The dotted lines are my leaps of faith."

"Let me see how the money lines up," Ravi said as he retrieved his brother's laptop and hard drive. Once the computer was up and running, the drive started to whir away as they buried deeper and deeper into each connection. They searched each reference point on Sophia's map until they drew each financial relationship on top. The result was a view of the drug world that had never been seen before.

Can this really be correct? Ravi thought but couldn't bring himself to ask.

Before them on the table was a scheme that saw governments backing the financial risk of the drug trade while the Catholic Church retained the profit. From recovery programs to halfway houses, the Catholic Church took in huge sums from parishioners and governments alike. With the religious market-share controlled by the Catholic Church, the police and military weren't on the take: They were paying the Catholic Church while doing the Catholic Church's bidding. When cartel bosses paid off the police and military, the officers gave that money to the Catholic Church and the Catholic Church gave it right back to the cartel bosses. When one region needed to bring down a cartel boss or intercept a large shipment so that a government official could gain more credibility and public appeal, the Catholic Church turned out the one to be caught.

Each parish ran like a mob Laundromat. Unsuspecting parishioners put in small amounts of clean money to make the system look clean. Large amounts of dirty money lined the pockets of government officials to ensure the small money kept coming, and because these people were parishioners as well, the amount of dirty money that they made clean through their donations was bigger. The Catholic Church knew who had drug problems, who had money problems, and who could be blackmailed, and these people became the mules, the fall guys, and the small time dealers. These people, the most vulnerable of each society, became the slaves that kept the big money flowing. The dirty cash reserves were constantly being invested in more jungle factories filled with parishioners who gave their money right back to their employers through the Catholic Church. The dirty cash reserves were constantly being invested in more dirty politicians, dirty police, and dirty military officers who gave their money right back to the Catholic Church. The dirty cash reserves were constantly being invested in the drugs that had to be caught, the cartel bosses that had to be paraded through the media after a successful bust, and the communities that had to be saved from the violence and havoc of drugs that then furthered a need for investment into the Catholic Church.

The Catholic Church was not skimming off of the top in the drug game. The Catholic Church was the drug game.

The Catholic Church orchestrated the small-time game of whack-a-mole that everyone was watching on television. It knew who would be caught because they put those criminals—their criminals—in the path of those officers—their officers. Around one percent of gross domestic product was being paid to the Catholic Church as tithes; the black and white map in front of Ravi and Sophia showed that the Catholic Church influenced, and nearly controlled, just less than one-fifth of the Central and South American economies.

"This makes my conversation with Angus a bit clearer," sighed Ravi. The darkest part of the night was past, and the sky was beginning to settle into the perpetual haze of a grey, Scottish winter morning. Ravi looked out his window back towards the science center along the River Clyde. Within his view were no less than three steeples, one mosque, and one Sikh temple. Each of these structures stood beckoning people of various faiths to seek fulfillment, peace, and salvation. All over the world, this dream of salvation played out in neighborhood after neighborhood. Ordinary, hard-working people hoped for more than the life they were living. These people went on faith, a faith built stronger by these structures, and followed their leaders towards a dream they could not see on their own. And here, in the early Scottish morning in a Partick apartment, it was finally as clear to Ravi that their leaders were preying on this faith. They were abusing their trust. They were stealing salvation.

"What did he say?" Sophia asked quietly as she watched Ravi at the window.

"This must be only a piece of the puzzle." He wanted to tell her more, but putting this together with the information Angus had provided seemed too far-fetched. His logical brain could not help but censor his mouth. "He said that the Orange Order is essentially an arm of the Catholic Church designed to create violence so that the Catholic Church can make money running weapons. It sounds pretty fantastical, but when it is staring at you in black and white...I don't know."

"Sometimes the worst truths are so amazing that you can't make yourself believe them," shuttered Sophia. "Can I stay here today? I'm not sure I can face this alone."

Chapter 4

Ravi awoke in darkness to a persistent knock at the door. He sat forward in his chair to see Sophia sleeping on the couch under his coat. As the caller knocked again, Ravi glanced at his watch: it was only half-nine. Rubbing the sleep out of his eyes, he cautiously cracked the door to see a grinning young man in the hallway.

"We need to grab a drink," the young man said cheerfully. While he was clearly American, he had an odd, half-Irish accent. Ravi looked back towards Sophia, debating her safety before it struck him that his own was also in question. "She'll be fine." As if he could sense Ravi's hesitation, he added "Don't forget, her safety is our decision at this point. And I can assure you, she will be fine while we're having a few beers."

With no more than a heavy jumper on, Ravi followed the man down the stairwell and into the biting chill. "Might need a few to warm up once we're there," Ravi commented, hoping to quell his fears that were now making him shiver more than the winter wind.

"Have as many as you'd like. I've got all night," the young man smiled back. Ravi jumped at each passing car thinking one would pull up to drag him away. "We're almost there; it's just here on the right."

Ravi had passed Stumps Bar for years but had never considered going in. It just didn't look like his kind of place then, and it sure didn't look like his kind of place now. It felt as if every eye in the bar was on him from the moment he crossed the threshold. "Just grab those seats in the corner there. Lagers are fine, I assume?" It was a traditional pub in every sense from the large gold letters on the red header above the door, to the tweed upholstery and dark wood furnishings. There were still a few old couples who had been there since early afternoon, the kind that come in every day around three o'clock, order lagers and shandies, and avoid seeing each other for the remainder of the night. The older couples were being replaced by younger ones at this point. A few of them were not yet into the routine of dating, and a few more were well on track to replacing their elder versions in the bar. As with everything in a pub like Stumps Bar, grime piled upon grime, the smell of stale lager built upon the stagnation, and the former generations saddled their habits upon the next generation. The only thing that progressed in a bar like this was time, yet few patrons realized the true cost of each pint.

"Eh…sure; that works." Truth be told, Ravi was not a huge fan of Tennents, but it didn't really seem like the time or place for any special orders. Most Americans that came to Scotland expected to find an exclusive, little known beer that they could claim as their own when they returned home. They hoped for something like the Scottish equivalent of VB, but most settled for Tennents as the most popular options around here were Bud Light, Miller Genuine Draft, and Stella.

Ravi looked back into the room from the empty corner seats. Every glance that came his way felt like a threat. Every new person coming in the door was sure to be the hired gun that would blow him away. When the American came back, he was carrying one pint and one closed can with a glass balancing on top. "I was assuming you'd be suspicious of any beer already in a glass; thought I would try and put your mind at ease." Until that point, poisoning had never even crossed Ravi's mind. His show of good faith terrified Ravi even more.

"I'm not sure what they say over here, but we're told in the US that you should never talk about politics, religion, or sex on the first date," he said as he took a sip of his beer. The only break in his smile came when the glass touched his lips. If they had seen each other on the street, Ravi would have identified him as any other politician or salesman. Here, he just felt dangerous. "I was hoping we could break all three of those rules tonight." He shot out his hand toward Ravi. "Not saying I'm buying you drinks to have sex with you, of course." The grin accompanying this little joke was infectious, and Ravi felt himself relax slightly with the man's effortlessly carefree manner.

"Glad we got that out of the way. Didn't want you thinking I'm some tart that shags any bloke who knocks on my door." Ravi snorted to himself, trying to shake off his tremors.

"Perfect. Let's start off with religion, then. I assume you're not Catholic?" The man drank as each pause allowed, but never broke his scan of Ravi. He studied Ravi's every move, his every facial expression, his every flinch, and his every twitch.

"Aye, that's a pretty safe bet."

"I'm not here to save your soul. Well, not tonight," he smiled. "But I am here to give a bit of advice that will save your life." There was an unmistakable change in tone, but his outward appearance remained as care free as before. "Right now, you are safe. Sophia is safe. Professor McKenzie is safe. You will go on with your life as normal. Nothing will be changing in the immediate future. But you have raised a few red flags, and I'll need you to ensure certain people see certain things a certain way. And this is where we begin to discuss politics."

"What do you mean by politics?"

"There are a number of changes afoot that the world does not suspect. I'm assuming you don't really follow the Catholic Church?"

"Not really," Ravi shrugged.

"Right now, a number of things are starting to align. I am a fixer, meaning I help them align in a manner that my boss needs. You present an issue to some, but I believe you stand here as an opportunity for us," he said before taking another drink of his beer. "The unpublished thesis that Professor McKenzie pulled up for you alerted us that you were getting into an area that we would rather keep shut. We have put a lid on it, as you can see."

"Can I ask a question?" Ravi broke in.

"Oh, yes," he appeared somewhat startled by Ravi's request. "Please, this truly is a two-way conversation. I am assuming we will end this conversation as partners, meaning I hope you will speak freely with me."

"Really? That seems a bit far-fetched, to be honest," Ravi replied as his eyes narrowed. This whole engagement was becoming strikingly surreal.

"Really. We will trust you with some very sensitive information. We will be doing this because you are currently safe, although we know how to change that in an instant." For the first time, his smile vanished. "That is a guarantee."

The man broke his stare by taking a drink, which made his smile return. "What do you know about the College of Cardinals?"

Ravi shook his head as he sat back for a moment. "Nothing, really: high level Catholics who dress in red. That's about it."

"Well, that's sort of it," said the man. "The funny thing about the position of Cardinal is that it's not actually a supervisor on the organizational chart. While most are Bishops, they don't need to be, so you can find a lot of freedom in selecting the right person for the right job."

"Okay, so..."

"How familiar are you with Cardinal Turkson?" Ravi shrugged. "He's from Ghana, very popular, plenty of support for many reasons. The majority of those reasons are sitting on the USB drive that Angus gave you."

"Come again?"

"Don't act stupid. I know what Angus gave you in the same way he knows what happened to Professor McKenzie," the man said with a hint of irritation through an expanding smile. It was unclear if the smile was to emphasize the irritation, or mask the pleasure of sitting in the Puppet Master role at the table with Ravi. "You came up on our watch list because of what the Professor showed you, and the Royal Black put him under for safe keeping because we need him there."

"Who's the 'we' you keep referring to?"

"As I mentioned, I am a mere fixer. I was born and raised in South Boston. You know, Good Will Hunting? My boss is publicly charged with fixing the sex abuse scandal. His role is to contain it, make sure it doesn't go somewhere it can't go. If it goes into certain areas, we cannot control a range of bigger issues, so his role is to give the public their red meat, give them the blood they are looking for, while keeping the heart in place. That's where you present a clear and present risk," his smile was back to normal. "But it is also where you present us with an opportunity. Someone who knows they need a way out is often willing to take what you offer them. I offered you the information on that drive."

"Angus said not to use it until I was ready, but I have no idea what it is. How will I know when I'm ready?"

"I'll tell you when you are ready. For right now, it is the ace up our sleeve." With another drink, he was finished. "You drinking up, or will I be doing all the drinking tonight?" He walked to the bar, ordered another, and came back a sip down so as not to spill in transit.

"You remember what Angus told you about the Orange Order?" He said as he sat down again.

"Aye. And to be honest, it sounded ridiculous."

The comment seemed to almost offend the man who crumpled up his face and cocked his head at Ravi for a moment. "Why is that?"

"The Catholic Church is running weapons? That doesn't make sense."

"When was the last time you saw a leopard change its spots? You are what you are, kid." The man nearly chuckled at Ravi's disbelief. "The Church has been dealing in weapons since the days of Joshua at Gilgal. What do you think the Crusades were? Someone had to outfit all of those soldiers. It's not like our ancestors perfected such a profitable technology just to watch it be given away. The Catholic Church has been in the weapons game since before its founding.

"What has changed is the scale of it and where we make our money now. This is what brings us to Cardinal Turkson. He is the Cardinal appointed to oversee that aspect of the Church's business." He paused to gauge Ravi's reaction, as if he was trying to see how much Ravi really knew. "There are pieces of our current trade that can be attached to Cardinal Turkson personally, and there are pieces that can't be found. We want to keep the head safe by lobbing off the arm that everyone sees."

As they talked, Ravi's phone began to vibrate. He slid it far enough out of his pocket to see that it was Sophia before letting it go to voicemail.

"You need to get that?"

"No, it'll be fine."

"Happy to let you take it if it is Sophia; she's probably worried."

"It's no problem," he replied. It made Ravi uncomfortable that this man, who had yet to offer Ravi his own name, knew that Sophia was sitting alone in Ravi's apartment right now. "I'm assuming I'll be home soon?"

"I'm here as long as you need, not a minute more," the man grinned.

"Then explain the Orange Order. I just don't get it."

The man crumpled his face again, and Ravi could see his eyes searching for where to start. "I'll start a bit further back. From Gilgal—are you familiar with Gilgal?"

"I assume so. Joshua launches his attack on Jericho from Gilgal and continues his conquest into Canaan. Is there more to it?"

"From that perspective, that is the basic roadmap. From the Church's perspective, Gilgal was the start of its weapons business. In the same way, Moses, Joshua, and all that followed were really military leaders who found God; their support network of arms makers, dealers, and carriers were their congregation. It's no different than most religions. We're a community first, and heaven just happened to appear. You Sikh?"

Ravi nodded, not sure what the man was trying to get at.

"You guys were a little different in structure and origin. All of those protestant sects were a bit freer to actually find God, even if it confused the main issue. True Christianity and Islam, however, were both organizations of necessity and the religion became a pastime of convenience that kept everyone in line. After all, who would trek through the desert for years to go murdering people if god weren't involved? Then again, what else are you going to do in a desert?"

Ravi sat back in his chair. If he was hearing this correctly, the Catholic Church was nothing more than a front for various illicit operations that justified its existence by perpetuating a concept of God to its constituents. "So what does this have to do with the College of Cardinals?"

The man waived his head back and forth, thinking through the best way to put it. "Think of the Cardinals as the advisers to the CEO. Most of them are Presidents of their division, some of them aren't, but each of them is assigned areas of responsibility. Cardinal Turkson's area is the weapons trade. Like every President, he got his hands dirty before he was put in charge, and, like most Presidents, he has his sights set on the top job."

"So are we taking down Turkson in favor of your guy?"

The man's grin widened. "Now you're starting to get the politics of it. Good job, kid." The man gave a quick raise of his eyebrows in sarcastic approval before moving on. "My boss prefers the king maker role. We're interested in a North American future, but we can do more from Boston than Rome."

"But isn't it too soon to worry about electing a new Pope? The current Pope seems young and in excellent health. A lot can happen in the years to come."

"Executing the timing of it all is my job. I can assure you, we know what we're doing on our side. We've done it for centuries now and will continue for centuries more." He glanced at his watch before looking around the room, as if he was waiting for someone else. After a quick scan his attention was back with Ravi. "This is where we need you to be clear on what you are doing. The reason Turkson is in his role is because he cut his teeth in Rwanda and the other sub-Sahara wars and genocides. He was, and is, a skillfully ruthless operator. He will cut a throat before he cuts a price. He's impressive. The problem is, just like in the US Air Force, the organization focuses on the interests of the leader. Do you know what I mean here?"

Ravi shook his head, but the man was already off to his next point.

"For decades, the head of the US Air Force had been a fighter pilot. For that reason, the Air Force kept investing in fighter planes. But you watch Obama now: He's not calling in fighter planes. The world has changed. Al Qaeda doesn't have a bunch of MIG's playing out some Top Gun scene. They have a bunch of guys running around the desert, shitting on roofs, and burying homemade bombs. Fighter planes won't do anything for that." He shook his head to himself, as if he had fought those battles in those rooms with those generals just to watch them ignore reality. "You then put a cargo guy in charge; drones take off and success becomes attainable again. We are staring down the same issue here."

"What do you mean? Is the Catholic Church selling drones?"

"Well, yes. But that is not my point," he looked around again, as if someone should be entering on cue. "Direct focus on the weapons trade is not a high margin strategy for the coming decades. The world is awash in guns, bombs, and rockets. We will stay profitable in that business, but we will not really grow. Turkson doesn't get that. He's not a stupid man, he is just ignorant."

Ravi leaned back, resting his head against the wall. The whole thing seemed to take him in circles. "So what is the next growth business?"

"No one has said it better than Adam Smith. To badly paraphrase the great Scottish thinker: People are the only real commodity." His nod was short and consistent: the kind that was intended to get everyone else agreeing to something they didn't truly understand. "We humans go in cycles, swinging back and forth between the importance of things verses people. People are on the upswing, and our ability to trade in people has never been greater. That is where we will grow as an organization."

"What do you mean by the ability to trade in people? Are you saying that you see a rise in membership on the horizon?"

"Of course not. Membership will keep decreasing. That is just a fact of our current environment." He looked around again, saw a man who had come in, and appeared to stop looking. "Human trafficking is the current growth area. We're currently straightening out a few of our managers in this product line, but the number of managed assets will keep increasing. We just can't lose focus by fooling ourselves about where the market is going."

There was something about the last two lines that sounded so clinical. It was hard to think of the Catholic Church in terms of market share, revenue units, or strategic growth. It was hard to see its mission executed by a CEO with Presidents, middle managers, and managed assets. It was hard to imagine that a business which passed the hat each Sunday could be so financially influential in so many modern economies. It was hard to believe that what everyone saw in morning mass was only the tip of the iceberg. It was all just so hard to believe.

"I'm still not sure I understand the part about the Orange Order."

"The short of it is that you don't sell weapons without conflict. If you follow American politics: Eisenhower said America should be wary of the military industrial complex, but, having factories, facilities, and suppliers in every legislator's home district made it very hard for anyone to vote against it. To keep justifying spending money on those things, there needs to be conflict. While the Bush administration did a great job of manufacturing a war of choice, few administrations have been able to be so brazen.

"It is the same with us. We make the military industrial complex look tame. Every legislator has a connection to military developments, but we have a whole network that actually buys into what we do even when they do not fully understand it. We have decision owners who are, essentially, investors in our seen and unseen causes. But we also recognize that only having Catholics would have kept us out of the American political system, although the Church originally sought out a protestant element for the purpose of driving enough conflicts to make real money in the weapons business; image just how short lived Northern Ireland would have been if we hadn't been able to continually stop and restart the conflict. The Orange Order does have a few secrets that it considers its own, and it guards them effectively. A few were given to the Order; a few were found for it. At this point, very few people in any of those associated organizations even know why they are doing what they do anymore. They don't even know which of their actions are in or against their own interests. Much of it was luck, but it has worked out beautifully. Never underestimate the power of God," he smiled, as if the whole thing were just one big joke.

"So it was all planned? This distributed model where the right hand never knows what the left is doing?"

The man waved his head back and forth, looking again for the best words to explain a cloudy truth. "Yes and no. We didn't actually invent the approach. We've never really ever started anything. We're a bit like Apple; we see what works, steal it, and perfect it. In the same way that Toyota killed Detroit with its own innovations, we, for example, are now profiting in the Middle East using what they taught us. In a way, it is actually fun," he said as he looked through Ravi to admire his own professional successes.

"So, again, what exactly do you need from me?"

His smile dropped for only the second time. "You've seen what we needed to do to Professor McKenzie in order to ensure that line of business stays where it is. My boss cares little about what you do so long as he is allowed to continue burying it the way we are now. As long as that remains on track, we are happy enough. If you want to stop looking over your shoulder, we need to make sure that any discoveries you have made achieve some public notoriety that is focused on the contents of the USB drive Angus gave you. We have provided everything you need to connect Cardinal Turkson to genocide. That needs to be known, and it needs to happen on our schedule."

Ravi slowly nodded his head, and the man allowed his request to sink in.

"Don't worry, you'll know what we need and when." With a nod, a man across the bar got up and left. Without making eye contact, he finished their meeting with, "While I said that I was here for as long as you needed, I'm assuming this is as long as you need." He turned back to capture Ravi's eyes one last time with a half grin. "This will be a fun partnership. I look forward to working together."

He stood up as he finished his pint and set the glass down. "Keep warm," he said, and he walked into the darkness.

***

As Ravi left the pub, his mind was spinning. He had never even thought about the world his brother lived in every day: a world where the truth was always in the middle of lies and any mistake could be your last. It was all so new to him and he couldn't tell if it was the beer or the fear that was keeping him warm now. The car was almost on him before he even knew it was near.

"Oy, mate..." Ravi heard coming from the dark Peugeot. A window was coming down and a door was opening. Ravi's heart began to race as a bald head emerged from the driver's side door.

RUN!

He ran through the first opening that got him off of the street; it was a driveway to the back of a tenement block. His dress shoes were far from ideal for running, and he felt every step through the leather soles as the impact shot up his calves and into his knees. He lost traction running around the corner and slid on a knee as he scrambled to keep moving. Glancing over his shoulders he saw headlights coming down the alley. Looking around him he saw a wooden fence separating the parking lot from the railroad tracks. Seeing no other option, he ran to scale the fence.

His first attempt to jump the fence barely got him half way. His feet kicked and slid down the wet wood, and he heard a car stopping behind him. In moments they would be on top of him. "Oy, where do you think you're going?" he heard as he leaned forward and managed to fall over the top of the fence. He hit the ground face first, clawed at the dirt until the rest of his body was lined up to run, and raced up the hill towards the top of the tracks. Whoever was behind him was yelling after him. All he needed to do was get over those tracks, and he could disappear into the streets beyond them.

The red rock along the track bit at his hands, and it wasn't until the wave of wind escaping the northbound train hit him that he realized what the metallic whining, popping, and crackling below him was. He fell back from the oncoming train into the southbound tracks. He sat hovering above the tracks in a crab-like position, looking around and taking stock of what was behind him. All of the cars were in spaces, and he wasn't sure if one of them was the car from the road. A few people were still yelling something to him from the fence, and curtains were being pulled back all along the tenements for people to peak out at the growing spectacle.

He scrambled up to continue his attempted escape. He allowed himself to wince as his knee struck the tracks but forced himself to fight through it and scamper down the far side of the hill. He pulled himself over another fence and fell into the landscaping on the far side. He noticed that his hand was bleeding; his chest felt bruised like he had been run over; his knee was throbbing so hard that he wasn't sure if he could continue running. He clenched his eyes shut, forcing the pain to the back of his skull, and rolled onto his feet. As he staggered into a run, he looked across the Sainsbury parking lot for an exit. The alleys across Crow Road looked locked. The run to the left or right looked farther than he could manage right now. He raced for the road, hoping an opportunity would reveal itself when the police car stopped right in front of him. He froze as the constable flashed the blue lights and motioned for him to get in. When Ravi paused, the constable cracked the window, never breaking eye contact, as he calmly directed him to, "Get in the back, pal."

"Have a nice run?" the constable said as the car started up the road. His partner sat twisted in the passenger seat, watching Ravi through a set of unblinking eyes set within a face of stone. "I'm not sure you were paying attention earlier. You won't be hurt right now." Ravi sat there in the middle of the back seat with his bloody hand likely staining the fabric and his knee jammed up against the back of the driver's seat. He was no more than one lunge away from each constable's belt. Of course, he wasn't sure where that would put him. There were no handles on the doors for him to get out, and he was no Jason Borne. He heard what the constable was saying, but it did not make him any more comfortable. "I'm not sure if this is making any impression on you right now, but it should. You know that there are cameras on every shop, every junction, and every bridge. We know that you are smart enough to realize that we can reconstruct both where you have been and anywhere you hope to hide."

They rode in silence until the car pulled up in front of his tenement entrance. The partner got out of the car and walked around through the headlights to open his door. Looking Ravi in the eyes through the rear view mirror, the constable said, "She's still there: worried, but not shaken. Her voicemail was asking where you are and if she should come find you. She got a text back already saying you are fine and will be home soon. You should really start replying more quickly. It will make her worry less."

Ravi sat there for a moment, dumb struck, as his partner held the door open. "Sorry about the blood in the car," he managed to mutter as he slid out.

"Nae bother. Isn't the first time and won't be the last," he grinned.

"Sleep well," his partner quietly instructed has Ravi passed. They locked eyes for a brief moment before the door was closed and the car disappeared.

The first thing Ravi wanted, and the last thing he expected, was sleep.

Chapter 5

It was nearly noon by the time Ravi opened his eyes. Sophia was making eggs in the kitchen. It was fortunate that he preferred scrambled because that was the only way she could make them; she never could figure out how to fry eggs without either making them crispy or breaking the yolks so they turned into scrambled eggs anyway.

He sat on the edge of the bed, trying to piece together the night before into a story he could rationally explain. Even though she was awake and holding the phone when he got in, he was too shook to speak. They sat in silence for nearly an hour; both just stared at the floor until he finally crawled into bed and she lay down on the couch for a strained few hours of sleep. As he walked through to the kitchen, she stopped and looked over her shoulder at him before turning back to the face the stove.

"So happy that you are up," she said, still focusing on the pan in front of her.

"That's me. Sunny side up," he croaked in reply. "Scrambled again?"

She grinned. It was sort of a normalizing circumstance for them: No matter how much they changed or how strange the world seemed to them, her eggs were still terrible. "I'll scramble you if you don't watch it," she joked as she scraped the egg film from the surface of the non-stick frying pan with a metal spatula.

"It's nae bother. I like the little charred bits you've got there," he smiled. He had an urge to hug her. He wanted to come up from behind and grab her around the waist. He wanted to hold her tight to his bruised body. He didn't know if the feeling was mutual, so he just stood there, inches away from her, and peered over her shoulder into the yellow and brown mess she was heating. "See? Just how I always liked it."

"You mean how you always got it."

"Same thing. As long as I'm not the one cooking, I like what I get," he joked.

She put the eggs onto the plate next to her and handed it to him. She glanced at Ravi before starting work on another batch of "egg toast" as Ravi always used to call it. It was just like old times. She pretended to be a short order cook, while he pretended to enjoy her cooking.

"I can't stop rethinking everything I thought I knew," she said in a simple, matter of fact manner. "As prepared as we supposedly were, I never imagined that I would be in the middle of something like this. And now it's too late."

Ravi felt the urge to hold her again. He wanted to tell her that he would protect her from the danger that was so clear to both of them now. He hesitated to tell her about what had happened to him the night before; he didn't want to scare her more than she already was, but she still sounded so strong and in control of her emotions: same stagnant, solid Sophia. After all that has happened, maybe she should be the one protecting me, he thought.

"It is too late," he said, staring at a small crack in the kitchen drywall. He sighed heavily before recapping the previous evening in as much detail as he thought he could handle re-living. He told her about being chased by the dark car because his knee was still throbbing, and he was clearly bruised and scraped, but he decided to leave out the part about getting a ride home from the police. That was the part that terrified him the most: the police were working for the people who would prefer to have him dead or silenced in an equally permanent way.

Sophia stared at him unblinking and vacant of emotion. She looked as if the fact that they were being hunted by a group of pissed off, drug-lord cardinals and their stooges had sunk in. She looked normal: no more affected than she was when working on any other sensitive project for MI-6.

"We will never have our lives back," Ravi said as he came to the end of his tale.

They sat in silence as Ravi let the reality of that statement sink in. Sophia pulled her phone out of the pocket of the sweatpants she had borrowed from Ravi's disheveled dresser. She stared at the screen for a few moments before typing a few words and quickly putting it back in the pocket. Ravi didn't ask what she was doing.

"I think I'm going to visit Dave today," Ravi mumbled.

"Are you sure you want to go out there?"

"I don't know. We're as safe out there as we are here. That part is clear," he shrugged. "You want to come with me?"

She looked at him blankly. She didn't look worried or frightened. She just looked tired. "Sure. Can we stop by my flat first? I would really like to change into some of my own clothes. Not sure your jerseys and trousers are flattering enough even for visiting a comatose friend," she said plainly.

***

They arrived at the Western Infirmary just after three in the afternoon and were led to David's room by a nurse who seemed eager to get away from her stack of paperwork. Desperate for some outside interaction, the nurse mentioned about how strange it seemed to her that David's mother had only come once early on in his hospital stay and from then on, only a single male visitor had come regularly. The male was there for every moment of the visiting hours: he came in at two, left at four, and came back again between six and eight. He never missed a minute.

When they reached David's room, the man was sitting in the corner watching the door. The nurse signaled them into the room before heading back down the hall to the nurses' station. The man got up slowly as if he was expecting someone else to walk in behind them. He looked Ravi and Sophia up and down before extending his hand to Ravi.

"Are you family?" he asked in a northern English accent. The voice was strikingly soft coming from the hard shell of a human there in front of them. He looked like he could be any thirty-something door man from Nottingham: a weathered face, abused body, and abrasive hands. But there was something about his demeanor that was soft or even gentle.

"I'm guessing you aren't either, then?" replied Ravi as he shook his hand.

"Can I assume you are Ravi?"

Ravi knew who had sent this man. "I assume you are here to ensure I follow directions?"

"No," the man said softly. "But, well...I guess...partially." His face twitched and shifted as if he was not completely set on his answers. "I am here for myself, first and foremost. I am here to try...to try to regain my life."

Ravi's brow furled as he stood there confused. He didn't know what to make of this person, of his motivations, and of his and Sophia's safety in this man's presence. As they sat there in silence, a security guard bowed his head through the door frame as he slowly passed the doorway. The security guard clearly made this man nervous and his nervousness sent Ravi into an internal fury of terror and adrenaline.

Sophia, not seeming to recognize the man's change in countenance at the presence of the officer, had moved to David's bedside where she gently touched his arm. She did not reach out with the softness of a lover, but the curiosity of one who could not believe what was before them. She stared at David lying there, connected to machines that were keeping him in a state of undead.

"Any chance we could do this elsewhere? Three Judges around the corner, maybe?" She remained fixed on David but her voice shook like it was trying to run away from the scene without her.

"That sounds like an appropriate bar..." mused Ravi as they left the room.

***

The Three Judges was nearly empty when they arrived, so they sat at the window with a view down Dumbarton. With each meeting, the setup became more familiar: another encounter with another man who was driving another agenda. The only thing that became less familiar was reality. The portrait of the world being painted in front of him was fighting with Ravi's view of what he had always assumed to be true, and he struggled to reconcile those views with the actual truth that was somewhere in the middle.

"I'm told that Danny has already visited you," he started. "Officially, I am here to reinforce what he spoke with you about."

"Which part? The message that we are safe as long as we follow orders?"

"Nobody is safe in our current predicament," he replied softly. His eyes drifted down as if that fact made him take stock of his own situation.

"I'm going to be honest, my guaranteed safety was the only thing I would have been happy to hear," Ravi retorted sarcastically.

"Then I have nothing but bad news for you. We are both searching for a clean exit, but it is clearly a long shot for both of us. I'm hoping we can, at least, work together for a fighting chance at doing something meaningful here."

Ravi looked at Sophia next to him. He had secretly hoped that she wouldn't stay so calm. He had hoped that her panic could validate the terror that was growing inside him. When Sophia didn't even blink, Ravi felt even more desperate.

"What is meaningful for you?" Sophia asked.

"My husband. That is the only thing that has meaning for me anymore." His eyes began to water. It became clear to Ravi that he was not the only desperate man at the table.

The conversation paused as each ordered a drink in turn. As the beers came, Sophia broke the silence.

"How did you meet your husband?"

"In the Church. He truly saved my life." Mark paused to steady his wavering voice before he continued. "I was an orphan sent to live in a church orphanage outside of Edinburgh. Priests were raping little boys nightly. Little boys like me. They had flocks, as they called them, which were basically their property. They would get drunk and gamble their flocks like poker chips, allowing each other to do anything they wanted with us. From raping us themselves to making us masturbate in front of them...to making us rape each other."

He shook his head and wiped his eyes as his mind drifted back to those unimaginable nights. "My husband got to know me and we fell in love, and he won me in one of those games. I was traded away by the now Archbishop of Edinburgh."

"Wait, your husband is a priest?" Ravi asked.

"Yes. He reports to Archbishop Diarmuid Martin of Dublin." Mark paused, apparently expecting some sort of reaction out of Ravi and Sophia that never came. "Have you been following the issues in the Dublin archdiocese at all?"

"No, this is all new to me, pal," replied Ravi, shaking his head.

"I have a little," Sophia interjected. "But I'm not sure I know what you're getting at."

"How are you two this deep and don't even know the basics?" At that moment Mark became the most terrified looking one in the group.

"By accident, really," Ravi said after a blank glance at Sophia. "I'm just a historical linguist."

"And I'm a linguist supporting modern anthropological studies," Sophia added.

"So why are they so scared of you? What have you found?"

"Who are you talking about?"

"Tommy doesn't just tour Glasgow for no reason. You must have something he needs." Mark's voice was nearly pleading. "What did you talk about?"

Ravi was baffled now. How does this guy know nothing about the conversation with Tommy? "Weapons sales was the bulk of it," Ravi replied cautiously.

Mark was clearly confused. "What? Why?"

Ravi glanced nervously at Sophia. Were these two guys not connected? Who was this guy now? Was this a test of Ravi's loyalty?

"Why don't you tell me why David is sitting in that hospital right now? I'm not sure I'm comfortable divulging anything more until I can understand that." Ravi took on the hardest tone he could, hoping his bluff would lead them to some sort of a stable footing.

They sat looking at each other for a few moments, each contemplating the safest move, both unsure how they got here, and who they were dealing with. "That sounds fair," Mark finally conceded quietly. "Your friend is in that bed because Tommy thinks you have some key that can blow the lid off of the Church's human trafficking business. And that is why I am here as well."

With a heavy sigh, Mark continued. "The Catholic church is the largest player in the thirty-eight billion dollar human trafficking business," Mark replied as if this was common knowledge. "My husband is Raymond Field, one of the two Auxiliary Bishops who were scapegoats for the child sex abuse that became public a few years ago."

"What do you mean by husband, and what does this have to do with trafficking?" asked Ravi. "I thought all of those cases were in the communities that the priests were serving?"

"The sex abuse that is publicly known is all local. Archbishop Martin is one of the many scapegoats who will be paraded out in the coming months. Archbishop O'Malley, Tommy's boss, is orchestrating the scapegoating because the Church is playing a diversion game to keep people from even considering what it is actually doing: selling sex slaves all over the world. Auxiliary Bishop Eamonn Walsh secretly married us years ago. That is why the Church picked him and Ray to blame and the Church has now essentially put blood all over their hands."

"What do you mean by that?" asked Ravi.

"To make sure they didn't blow the lid off of the trafficking business, they buried them deep in it. They now have all the books, but they are also now in a position where they would be held entirely responsible for everything. They are trapped, and I was hoping whatever you have that is powerful enough to land your friend in a coma could be used to free Ray."

Ravi sat back and exhaled. This was an interesting twist. "But I just still don't even understand the trafficking. How is the Church in that business?"

"It's my understanding that it always has been," Mark shrugged. "It is my understanding that the Church has been in the business since the Crusades."

87

"What do you mean by the Church being in the business since the Crusades?" Ravi said leaning forward as Sophia leaned back in her chair.

"My understanding from Ray is that the tribes that later became the founders of Islam were originally in the sex trafficking business in a big way. It was, along with drugs and weapons, Muhammad's primary business. It was Ali, Muhammad's nephew, who really began perfecting the business for strategic gain by providing the sex slaves to and then blackmailing through that relationship, leaders all over the crumbling Roman Empire. As the Catholic Church became more prominent, more and more priests were being targeted in the same way. Because of the rising influence of Muslims throughout the Church due to their sex trafficking, Pope Honorius I decided to muscle the Muslims out by running the Church's own sex trade. And as it does with most things, the Church ruthlessly went after market share. The Crusades were meant to destroy any competition in that space."

"So what are you hoping we can do?" Sophia asked.

"If you have information that can prove this is all going on, I think it is my only hope of freeing Ray before he gets too deep to get out." He looked at both of them as if he was praying they had what he assumed he needed. "I know it is a long shot, but I don't know what else I can do."

"If we did have anything, what would you plan to do with it? Just take it to the paper and hope everyone says 'oh, looks good, guess we won't send you all to The Hague'?" For a moment, Ravi was almost angry with him. This was really his plan? If everyone knows, everyone gets a pass?

Since when has the world ever worked like that? As Ravi's face tightened in frustration, he could see Mark's falling. In a long sigh, Ravi said, "I think we may have your missing piece."

"But answer me one thing," Ravi said. "What about the Archbishop of Edinburgh? You're telling me that you're completely over him? This isn't some gamble on us to even some score with him?"

"Cardinal O'Brien is already in line to go down, I am not worried about that," he shrugged. "I just want to be sure Ray is out before the ground moves."

"Are you telling me you believe in the rapture, or something? Aren't you a little old for that," Ravi scoffed. Once in a while, he couldn't help himself from sneering at believers.

Mark cocked his head and squinted as if he wasn't quite sure what to make of the comment. "Are you not seeing what is happening here?" He said to Ravi. "Everyone is jockeying for change in the Church. Anyone who is stuck on the back side of that transition will be in for another generation."

"What do you mean by transition? How do you know that?" Ravi asked, nearly panicking now.

"Because we are here now. Ratzinger is on the way out, and Cardinal Ouellet is trying to line up the votes to be next. That is why O'Malley is lining up the worst offending pedophiles to take falls. Ouellet is cleaning house in their sex trafficking business so that when he becomes the next Pope, they can start expanding the business in a big way.

It is basically a modern day version of what Ali did to Muhammad."

"Wait, what?" Ravi broke in.

"Muhammad was the Cardinal O'Brien of his day. He was nothing more than a drug addict working in the sex trade. O'Brien ran boys back when it was a small time operation. He skimmed a few off the top. He was actually nearly thrown to the wolves years ago when it turns out he had actually raped the son of a pretty prominent politician. So, the Catholic Church kept moving him up in an effort to remove him from the product. The Church wanted to make sure he was far enough away from the boys that he didn't expose the true business because he couldn't keep from shagging his flock.

"Muhammad was the same. Muhammad couldn't help raping the women and boys they were trafficking, not to mention the profits they must have lost in the drugs he both used and gave away for free. So Ali basically drugged him up like an ancient oracle, let him be the muscle when they had to push someone around, and turned him into a religious icon. After all, Muhammad was illiterate. It was Ali who wrote the first Koran. That wasn't an accident."

Mark took a long drink of his beer, put it down, and looked Ravi straight in the eye. "As someone who has seen the inside, the more than thirty billion a year in sex trafficking business that the Church is running could still grow significantly. It is scary to think what they could do if Ouellet were in the driver seat."

"But the Pope isn't even sick. Are you saying someone would actually take him out?" Ravi mused in disbelief.

"The gamesmanship going on now would not be happening if something wasn't afoot," Mark replied, as if Ravi's question really made no sense. "I can safely tell you that no single man has ever gotten in the way of Church business in the past."

"How much of this can you prove?" Sophia asked. "All of these stories of Muhammad, all of the drugs, all of the women: How do you know that isn't just some racist fantasy?"

"Because your friend is in a coma. That's how I know it is true," he replied sharply. "If the two of you are actually history experts, you should be able to find the exact same facts. What I'm telling you can be found. The young PhD student whose thesis you read is evidence that a dedicated scholar can find these truths. But that young scholar no longer walks among us, and your friend is growing closer and closer to that same fate."

"That is ridiculous," exclaimed Ravi. "You're saying that Dave pulling up that unfinished thesis is what landed him in the Great Western?"

"Do you really think all of the structures that brought us the Inquisition would just vanish? The Congregation for the Doctrine of the Faith is stronger than it has ever been. Why do you think Ratzinger was even elected? In this age of technology, the Church knows more about the average person walking the street than MI-6, the CIA, and the

KGB combined. The Church can get you anywhere, anytime, by any means necessary."

"Drink up," Ravi said before downing his pint. "You need to see what we have."

Chapter 6

The day had already turned grey and the sun was beginning to set by the time they climbed the hill to Ravi's flat. Sophia had pulled her red overcoat tight and turned her face down in an effort to brace against the wind. Ravi's eyes were wandering into the recesses of his brain, hoping to find a solution to their problem with the pieces they had now. Mark was constantly looking around, looking for any sign of danger. As they started to turn up the stairs, Mark leaned in and said to Ravi, "We won't be able to speak in your flat. Remember, I am only here to talk about the pedophilia issues."

"I understand," replied Ravi as he pulled the keys from his coat. "I just need to grab my laptop and we can head somewhere public."

"We should take the underground," Sophia announced. "It is almost impossible to track what anyone is saying, and everyone can see everyone. Any tape we ever got from the underground was nearly useless."

"Doing a lot of snooping on citizens, were we?" Ravi teased.

"Your brother did many things that shouldn't end up in the paper," Sophia replied coldly. "It's as safe as we'll get."

Ravi's heart jumped as he put the key in the lock. His mind ran wild with 'what-if' scenarios: What if someone was in the room? What if someone had come in and ransacked the place? What if the laptop was gone? With a few metallic clicks, he opened the door to find nothing out of the ordinary.

It was the only scenario he had not thought of.

As he cautiously entered the flat, he poked his head into each room to find nothing unusual. The bed was as disheveled as he had left it, the books were all on the shelves, and the kitchen was still as tidy as Sophia had made it. While Sophia went to the window to look out at the City, Mark milled around in the entryway. Ravi's computer was under the corner of his mattress, exactly where he had left it. He turned to leave his room as Mark appeared in front of him.

"You left everything you have on that computer here in this room?" he asked almost in a panic. "If that was there, they have everything. What were you thinking?"

"I was thinking that everything is actually on this drive," Ravi responded as he produced the hard drive from his pocket. "There is nothing on the computer itself."

Ravi looked at Mark for a brief moment, attempting to understand his expression, before walking past him into the living room.

"Oy, you ready to head out?" Sophia was as still as a statue staring out the window to the west. She took a slow, deep breath, and her exhale fogged up the window. "Are you ok?" Ravi approached her slowly, putting his arm around her shoulders.

For a moment, it was as if they were sitting on the grass of Gilmore Hill, looking down on the city. They had often sat on that hillside and admired the promise in the glorious city. In the spring, the sun would shine perfectly off of the science center, and the whole river would glow. He shared his fears with her, and she built up her hopes in him. It was almost as if he was not real if she was not depending on him. He needed to be her rock more than she needed a mooring. He truly had become nothing without her.

But then, they were on the same hill trying to figure out what the future held for them. "I'm not sure what you want me to do," she had said to him. "All you needed to do was be there for me. You're asking me to accept you after this?" he had responded. At the time, her betrayal was an insurmountable obstacle. Now, it seemed like it never even happened. He now longed for those lost years: those years in which he could have just seen past her infidelity. He could have just seen it as something he should have prevented. He could have just seen it as a cry for help in a relationship worth saving. But he didn't. "I can't trust you. And I'm not sure I ever can again." The door closed.

Sophia lightly trembled as if she were cold. "We're going to find a way out of this...will find some way to protect you." She continued to look out the window silently. "I promise. I will not lose you twice."

She turned her head to look at him; she had no sense of peace in her eyes. He kissed her gently on the forehead and squeezed her tightly before whispering that they had better go. "Let's go find our way out of this mess."

He looked back at Sophia when he reached the door. "Sophia?"

She turned slowly from the window and Ravi saw one bead of sweat drop from her forehead and onto her cheek. She slowly followed him out the door, staring at the carpet.

***

There are few things more distinctively unique than the smell of the Glasgow Underground. Any uninitiated passenger is overpowered by a historic cacophony of smells that have intermingled to create a distinctive odor with singularly indescribable qualities. It is as if generations of spilled drinks, vomit, urine, and mold have combined in a yellow tiled basement bathroom and grown into their own radiating concoction within the grouting. The only relief anyone get from the smell comes either as the hot air arrives before each approaching train or after time has dulled the senses to the point where the stagnant air at each platform seems normal.

The Underground tube is one big circle. No matter where you get on, fifteen stops later you are back where you started. Nearly once every year, Ravi would do the "Orange Donut" drinking game with his mates from the Union. Both the map of the tube and the trains themselves were bright orange, although more standard beige trains were continually appearing. On the "Orange Donut," they would each buy a Discovery pass, get off at each stop for a pint, get back on the next available train, and hope they made it home in the end. They had never paid much attention to the direction they started the tour until David got glassed late one night in Govan. Ever since that day, they would take the inner loop from Hillhead to get the Govan and Ibrox stops out of the way before all the neds came out.

As the three of them came down the steps into the Partick station, a bright orange train was just approaching. Unlike the London Underground, the platforms in Glasgow never feel even wide enough for the trains, and the tubular cars are barely tall enough for an average-height person to stand up straight if they are in the very middle of the car. The doors opened to a nearly empty car and they ducked in and sat on the brown and beige seats. As the train accelerated up to speed, the combination of track noise and rushing wind made verbal communication nearly impossible, while mobile service was only partially effective for brief moments as the train passed through shallower reaches of the system. Ravi opened the laptop, plugged in the drive, and they began to look for a glimmer of hope in the midst of the gathering darkness.

As the spider map pulled up on the screen, Mark's eyes widened. "Bloody hell," he nearly yelled over the din. "What is all that?"

"It's your husband's employer," Ravi shouted back. "These lines represent centuries of communications. We just don't know how to use it to our advantage."

"Can you search for key words?"

Ravi shrugged and nodded like a bobble head.

"Search for Fatima."

As the summary of every relevant document came up, the list grew from around the seventh century through the present. "There is more to her than meets the eye," Mark shouted. "She was Muhammad's whore before she was his daughter."

As they sped from stop to stop, arriving back where they started every 24 minutes, Ravi and Mark scoured the string. Fatima first came up in a sales receipt created by Ja'far in which she was described as only months old, and she surfaced again nearly a decade later in a purchase order that showed Ali buying her back in Medina. Mark and Ravi attempted to shout their discoveries to each other, jabbing at the screen to signal new searches, or leaning back to soak in the unexpected.

Chasing down every key word in Ja'far's purchase orders, Mark drilled into every road that ended with Fatima until he finally sat back with a contemplative grin. He pointed to a single name on the screen: Anicius.

"We need to find a place to talk," he shouted. With St Enoch's station coming up, Ravi closed the laptop and the three of them exited into the night.

With the lights of the late night holiday shopping still blazing up Buchanan Street, they stopped for a moment in St. Enoch's Square to consider their options. "Can we find somewhere public that has a few private corners? Some food may not be a bad idea, either," proposed Mark.

"Corinthian?" offered Sophia.

"Sure," replied Ravi, and Sophia began to lead the way. "So what is so important about Anicius?"

"Don't suppose you read any Dan Brown novels, do you?" joked Mark. "The irony of his work is that he stumbled so closely to the truth," he said with a wide grin. "Anicius is Pope Gregory the first, the man who essentially labeled Mary Magdalene a prostitute. If Dan Brown had actually connected a few dots instead of repeating some French dribble, he would have known that Mary Magdalene actually returned to Bethany after the crucifixion to have the third daughter of her and Jesus' five children. She never was Jesus' wife, but she was a revenue stream for the early Church just like plenty of other women."

"So you are saying that Mary Magdalene was actually a prostitute?" interjected Sophia. Ravi noticed that she was putting her phone into her jacket pocket.

"Aye. The money raised to support each Apostle's proselytizing typically came from selling offspring that they fathered on their journeys. They would typically recruit prostitutes, make them disciples, as Jesus did with Mary, and these women became traveling baby factories. The children were sold as children of God, often to communities where they would be used as sex slaves for the leaders to create offspring that were descendants of God. Every Christian foothold from the Colossians to the Romans was doing this.

"It was Anicius that acknowledged that Mary was a prostitute because he was the one who organized the operation under the roof of the Catholic Church. And this is where Dan Brown got so close, but missed the most mind blowing part," Mark said with a grin. "What you have right there is evidence that Fatima is truly the daughter of a prostitute from Jesus' bloodline."

The statement brought Ravi to a halt in the middle of the street. Mark was so lost in his own excitement that it took another three steps before he turned to wait for Ravi to process it all. "In the novel there is some secret society that is protecting the secret of Mary…"

"That's all bullocks," Mark cut him off. He put his hand on Ravi's elbow and tried to lead him forward toward Corinthian. "The whole Priory of Sion and all the French connection stuff is just a bunch of Muppets playing make believe. But there is an element within the Church that is now protecting Fatima's blood line. If we can find evidence of who they are, that will be our ticket out." There was a little spring in his voice, as if spilling the beans on such a large secret was enough to make them untouchable.

"Are you bloody joking?" Ravi could feel his blood boiling up in his face as his hopes fell to the pavement. "Your solution is that we release the equivalent of a Dan Brown novel? What kind of a silly cunt are you? Who the fuck do you expect to believe us? Is that the magic bullet you were searching for?"

"You have it there in black and white!" Mark argued. "If we release a few little pieces to the right people, they'll have to let us go to keep the rest hidden!"

"And who do you think are the right people? How do you think we know them?" Ravi said growing more anxious with every word.

"Ravi, calm down, please," Sophia said soothingly. "Maybe this can be a solution. Maybe Angus can help?"

Angus? Why would she bring up Angus? "I'm not sure if he would be the best person for this type of story, do you?"

"Maybe this is the type of thing that could help him?" she proposed. "Maybe this is the type of favor that protects his interests?"

"Who is Angus?" Mark asked softly like someone trying not to get in the middle of a domestic tiff.

"He is a reporter I used to work with," answered Ravi without taking his eyes off of Sophia who was looking at her phone hidden behind her coat sleeve. Who was she texting?

"Why can't he help us, Ravi?" prodded Mark.

"I'm not sure," replied Ravi. "I guess we'll see."

***

Corinthian was a collection of bars and restaurants packed into one of the most stunning four-story buildings in Glasgow. Sophia led them downstairs to the Mash and Press Rooms in the basement.

The bar feature was vaulted and the brick ceilings were supported by imposing stone pillars. The room was nearly empty when they arrived; only the staff was bustling around in preparation for the evening's onslaught. They sat down at one of the tables and opened the computer again. "Now, what are we looking for?" asked Ravi.

"Ray says that there is a group within the sex trafficking business that supplies to high value customers, like politicians, bankers, or other world leaders. Rumor has it that this group uses prostitutes from the Fatima bloodline," he said. "Maybe connecting the dots between that group and a few politicians will be enough of a bargaining chip for us to get out of this mess."

Ravi looked at Mark, then Sophia, and back at the computer. "Let me get this straight: We're going to uncover evidence that the Catholic Church is blackmailing politicians, as it has done for hundreds of years now, using prostitutes that are descendants of the Prophet Muhammad and Jesus Christ the Lord and Savior. And once we uncover this, they are just going to let us go. Is that the plan?"

Sophia did not make eye contact with Ravi. Mark nodded slowly. "I'm not sure there is a better plan," Sophia nearly whispered, looking down at her hands in her lap.

Ravi shook his head as he continued to type and watch the spider map on his screen. With every key word he entered, the map shifted like a net drifting towards its intended prey. He combed through various leads from the C Street House to the Order of Mary Magdalene. With every search, the scale of the conspiracy became more ominous. The connections were so broad until Ravi noticed something unusual.

"The number of connections to MI-6, the CIA, even the FSB...they are..." As he started to refine the searches further, the net began to tighten. "These are actually flowing through..."

"Fancy seeing you here." Ravi looked up to see Angus standing at their table, drink in hand. "Not sure we've met? Angus," he said with an outstretched hand.

"Mark."

"Mark. Where you from, Mark?" Angus asked as he sat down. Ravi turned his attention back to the screen in front of him, feverishly attempting to make sense of his closing net.

"Dublin."

"Funny, I'd place you in Leith."

"Well, I am from Leith, though I've been living in Dublin for a few years now."

"Fancy that. Tell me what you do there, Mark?"

Mark was silent for just a moment too long. Ravi looked up to see his eyes darting from person to person. "I'm currently on the dole, really. My wife works outside the home."

"If I was a betting man, and if they ain't ponies, I ain't bettin', I'd say you are in the employ of the Catholic Church." Mark sat there, mouth agape, at a complete loss for words. "You look like a churchy kind of bloke to me," Angus continued, pointing his drink holding index finger at him like a drunken prosecutor. "What say ye to that?"

"I'm not sure why you would say that…"

"I had a dog once," Angus spoke over Mark. "It was a mangy little scavenger dog, the kind that homeless people have. And it loved to eat shite. As hard as you would try to head it off, it would find any morsel of shite and have it down its throat before you could even yank its chain."

Angus took a drink from his glass and continued.

"You don't want your dog to eat shite because they can catch diseases and the like from them. If a dog eats the wrong shite, you lose the dog. But some dogs, you just can't train it out of them. Many a time, I'd jam my fingers down the dog's mouth in an attempt to tickle its throat if I caught it in time. I'd pull my hand out, fingers covered in shite, but the dog had already gotten his treat. Supposedly, if you can make it so uncomfortable for the dog every time it eats shite, it will stop eating shite. Seemed odd to me, but I'd suppose if someone repeatedly jammed a nob down my throat, I'd stop being gay."

Ravi stopped typing and looked at Mark; strangely, he didn't look in the least bit shocked.

"So I did my best to keep the dog from eating shite," Angus continued as if trying to get a reaction out of Mark. "But I could never quite keep it on the straight and narrow. One day the dog went for a big one behind a doocot, and before I knew it, the pup had choked down some junkie ned's turd and half the Buckie bottle that was broken beneath it: sliced the dog's insides from throat to stomach, and it died there along the canal coughing up bloody shite."

104

Angus sat up, finished his glass, and looked over his shoulder to the waitress. The bar was starting to fill up now, but she still came straight over to exchange his empty for another full, clear drink with no ice.

"Speaking of dogs chasing shite, I've heard stories that this man was a powerful academic at one point, but I've never seen him with a computer out in a bar before." Angus was looking at Ravi, half grinning. "Why would someone come to a doocot with a computer?"

"Just wrapping up my latest television commercial. It features three blind rats," Ravi replied dryly.

"Does the farmer's wife still catch their tails?"

"Not sure yet. I've only gotten through the dialogue. I was thinking it would go squeak, squeak, squeak. Squeak, squeak. Squeak, squeak, squeak."

Angus snorted and nodded as he drank again. "Sounds like a winner. You've really grown up as an artist."

"So what types of birds are we chasing tonight boys?" Angus turned side to side to scan the room before refocusing back on Mark. "I think it was Ravi here that turned me onto this fact first, but we Scottish don't know how good we have it. We live in a land of baps, present company excluded," he said, nodding towards Sophia. "Birds here are like icebergs. You think you're heading home with an A-cup just to find and arm full. We must be the only place in the world where bras are reinforced with steel cables. But we just don't appreciate it.

105

"Like that one over there," he said, pointing to a girl at a table across the room. "She's probably fresh from the Borders, in town to go to Uni, and out in the new center of her world.

"Do you know what they call a virgin in Galashiels?" He paused for a moment, staring at Ravi who had heard the joke a million times before. "Any wee lass 'at can run faster 'an her father. She doesn't look like a sprinter. That may be your doo there, Mark," he said with a nod.

"The next dog we had was a little older when we got 'im. When we brought him in the house, he started marking everything. That damn dog was pissing on anything he could lift his leg next to." Angus got up and started to move around towards Mark. "A neighbor said that if we chopped his bollocks off, he'd stop. So we did." He set his drink down and used both hands as if he was holding the dogs testicles in one hand and his other hand became a pair of shears. He snipped at the air like a drunken surgeon as he continued. "Snip, snip, snip, and he should have been cured. But you know what's funny about a dog with no balls? They mark even more."

Angus leaned menacingly over Mark, one hand on the table, the other hand japing at the air in front of him. "You know why? No? They are over compensating. When you take a man's balls..."

Angus's hand shot down and grabbed Mark's crotch. Mark doubled over against Angus's arm, clinging for support as his lips fought to keep his scream contained.

"They keep their bluster, but lose their fight. The smart ones know when it's time to bow out. But we had to put our dog down." Ravi watched Angus's forearm as the muscles slowly tensed, clenching his fist tighter and tighter until Mark looked like a man starved of oxygen. Angus finally released Mark but remained over him for a moment before silently sitting down again, clasped his hands on the table in front of him. "Maybe you should see if your little doo over there will kiss your booboo? We sure don't need any sterile dogs marking over here."

Silent and stoic, Mark got up from the table, picked up his glass, and walked to the other side of the room. Angus watched him for a moment before looking over his shoulder to the waitress and pointing to their table. "If you want out of this alive, it's time to make our move. I have prepared everything at the station. If we get there now, we should be able to do a quick interview, get it to all the morning news shows, and hopefully hide you in plain sight until we can find a safer long-term strategy."

Angus stood up, pulled on his coat, and before they had time to think about it, Ravi and Sophia were following him outside. They walked briskly along the streets up to the Buchanan Underground station through George Square. "I assume you have the USB I gave you the other day?" Ravi twisted his messenger bag around so that Angus could see into the inside pocket.

"I assume you are speaking for Tommy on this one?" Ravi asked.

"I'm speaking for you," Angus replied. "Tommy is no longer in this horse race."

George Square was already being decorated for the holidays. The foundations of the ice rink were laid, and the stalls were assembled. The air was crisp, and holiday shoppers strolled back out of the pubs where they wound down following the late night shopping excursions. Ravi reached down and squeezed Sophia's hand. For an instant, he felt as if they were just like any other couple strolling through George Square enjoying the shared passage of time.

The reality came back as soon as it left when they arrived at the opening to Buchanan street station. The air was warm, thick, and again smelled of the city's dirty history. Ravi only hoped that there was a light at the end of this tunnel.

Chapter 7

Once they had reached the relative calm of the platform, Ravi crouched against the wall and plugged in the USB. The computer spun up as the screen came alive with another trove of files. As he started to read through them, it became clear that weapons trafficking was not what Tommy expected him to find. Ravi looked up to see Sophia watching him while Angus paced uneasily, searching for a train in the tunnel's blackness. As Ravi met her eyes, uneasiness flowed through him like the vodka flowed through Angus. She looked at him as if the future was inevitable—as if she knew how this would play out. She looked at him as if she had put it all in motion.

As each file opened, the computer raced to translate it from Spanish to English. Communication after communication popped up, lists of names, places, dates, all being turned over to Videla or Massera by Cardinal Bergoglio. In return, bus routes, flights, ships, and even individual mules were identified as 'protected'. Cardinal Bergoglio traded priests, reporters, even parishioners against kilos of cocaine, heroin, and marijuana. As the spider map grew with every new document, the South American net began to reshape and close around Buenos Aires. In the same way that the sex trade began to center on Cardinal Ouellet and the weapons trade began to center on Cardinal Turkson, the spider map centered the drug trade on Cardinal Bergoglio.

As the ground rumbled with the approaching train, Ravi looked up at Sophia again to find her gaze unchanged. She just sat there looking at him as if she were looking at a memory. Ravi closed the laptop and they ducked into the orange train.

Ravi and Angus sat next to each other, and Sophia sat across the train. "You and I will get off at Kelvinbridge and head up to the station. Sophia can continue onto your flat. Does that work for you?" he shouted across the train. Sophia just nodded silently.

"What did you find on the USB drive?" Angus asked.

"I'm not sure," Ravi responded. "I think I need to know more about the Royal Black Institution."

Angus's mouth bent into a smile, his eyes studying Ravi in an attempt to break into his thoughts. "That's not a very wise topic. And I'm pretty sure that isn't what was on the USB."

As the train slowed into Cowcaddens, Ravi decided to call his bluff. "What I'm seeing is a web connecting MI-6, the CIA, and the FSB to the Royal Blacks and all of them are intimately tied to the sex trafficking business. Are these organizations all in on the conspiracy around the Fatima blood line?"

Angus just snorted as he shook his head. "Use your fucking head. Now is not the time to be a silly little cunt." Angus looked at the floor to gather his thoughts for a moment before looking back at Ravi. "Of course the Royal Blacks are protecting the Fatima blood line. It is a dangerously profitable collection of human assets. Even the most secular of politicians get uneasy when they find out they've been shagging both Jesus and Muhammad at

110

the same time. Can you believe what kind of power that is? The Royal Blacks is not the target of interest here, though. The business of human intelligence is a very dirty business, and it cuts both ways. You don't want to be in the middle of that. There is no one to protect you in that battle."

"So the Royal Blacks is essentially just an intelligence unit?"

"Don't be so daft. It is the intelligence unit. It defines intelligence. WMD? The Royal Blacks ended Tony Blair, not some American cowboy. The Royal Blacks define the playing field, they don't pick sides."

"But surely you must be on a side right now."

"Shockingly, I'm the only one on your side at the moment." Angus leaned in closer to whisper as the train began to roar down the tunnel again. "And I do mean the only one."

Ravi looked across the carriage at Sophia who was putting her phone away again. As she looked up, their eyes met for a moment, but she looked neither worried nor affected by anything.

"I just don't get it," Ravi deflated. "Is this some war of civilizations? Is this just a constant game of taking whatever is holy to one people and twisting it for the profit of another? Are all of these houses of worship truly just brothels for organized crime?"

"Ravi, it never was anything more. Spirituality was always a justification. God has always been on the side of the victor. The dead have no savior."

"But in our current turmoil with the Islamic world squaring off against the West, is it really as trivial as divisions within GE fighting for market share?"

Though he had spent decades working to prove the randomness of the world, Ravi was now begging and pleading for there to be more to it. "Are there really no great civilizations fighting for their honest vision of humanity?"

"There was a war of civilizations, Ravi, but that's all over," Angus smiled. "We won. These governments all run around doing the bidding of a man elected by criminals. The world is no more than what you take from it, and the Catholic Church is the only one taking. The rest of us are servants."

As the train began to slow down for the Kelvinbridge station, Angus stood up and nodded at Sophia. "We'll call on you as soon as we can. Wait in Ravi's flat until we know it's safe."

As they exited, Ravi stopped for a moment to look back at Sophia who sat watching him. As the doors closed, he watched flashes of her through the windows until the darkness swallowed the train whole.

They started for the stairs. "I'm concerned that the ground beneath us is shifting, Ravi," Angus said. His tone stopped Ravi in his tracks.

"What do you mean?"

"We laid the foundation for you to take down Cardinal Bergoglio. It troubles me that Kevin was brought in on

112

this." Angus's head was on a swivel, looking for anything out of the ordinary on the empty platform.

"Kevin?"

"Mark. He's actually Royal Black as well. I'm afraid the balance of power is shifting here." After climbing only a few steps, Angus stopped. Standing at the top of the stairs were five police officers flanking a man dressed in black. As one officer pointed down at the two of them, Ravi recognized the man in black from their encounter in the quadrangle just minutes before his brother's murder.

As the officers descended the stairs, Angus just watched them approach. "We're all the same, Ravi. We think it won't happen to us." The smile on his face was one of a poker player who had just gone all-in with a pair of sevens, just to watch his opponent call his bluff. "That's why we are chosen."

Fear started to surge through Ravi's body. With every beat of his heart, adrenaline coursed through his veins, and his feet grew light. As he looked at the officers descending, he started to panic. There must be a way out of this!

"Ravi, stay still." But that was no longer an option. His mind could hold no other option. RUN!

Ravi turned and ran for the tracks. Behind him he could hear the officers start to chase down the stairs. "Where do you think you're going?" Angus called out.

As children, Ravi and his brothers had explored nearly every inch of the City's cavernous underworld. For centuries, Glaswegians has created and destroyed catacombs, crypts, and tunnels for storing and moving everything from people to trains. An abandoned station was in the blackness ahead of him. If he could just make it to the station before the next train came, he could exit nearly anywhere in the City.

Behind him he could hear the officers stopping at the platform's edge while their radios crackled to life. He had only run this stretch of track once before when he was only seven years old. With every step into the blackness he prayed that his foot found flat ground. He had less than four minutes to make it to the next platform before the next train filled the narrow tunnel.

He could hear music in the tunnel ahead of him, but from behind, he felt the rocks on the tracks shake. Every ounce of fear turned into an extra burst of speed. His shadow began to appear on the walls in the train lights. The metallic screaming of the rails were now accompanied by the crackle and pop of the approaching train. Ravi was now fully in the train's sights and the abandoned platform was illuminated just meters ahead of him. The train's wheels began to screech and the cars began to bang and rumble as the conductor applied the brakes. He could feel the warm front of air catching him as he jumped onto the platform.

Before he could get completely clear, his left foot was struck as the train slid by him. The impact shot a stabbing pain through his every fiber as his body spun around before slamming to the cement floor.

He glanced up at the stopping train, watched the people inside as they looked at him in shock. In an otherwise uneventful evening, they were being thrown around unexpectedly and were completely unaware of why the world was shifting around them. Ravi tried to stand up but collapsed as the sharp pain in his foot brought tears to his eyes. As he tried a second time, he saw a little girl kneeled at the train window. She looked curious but no more affected than Sophia was just moments ago when Ravi left her in the train car. He stared at the girl for a moment before bracing for the pain and dragged himself to the edge of the platform and down into the abandoned tunnels.

The abandoned tunnels were used for everything from hide and seek to drinking and raving. While urban explorers dominated the tunnels each weekend, neds could be found drinking their Buckie and Tenants when avoiding school. Nights, however, were typically dominated by raves. Those who had never been submerged in the world of the underground would often find themselves walking down Great Western or Woodlands Road wondering where the hypnotic house music was coming from but never thinking to look down at the manhole covers. Every agonizing step brought Ravi closer to the pulsing music of what sounded like a rave that was at the height of insanity.

The crowd was between fifty and one hundred strong and three DJs stood on a makeshift stage of plywood and milk crates. Most were on their feet attempting to track the glow sticks in their hands, while some had given up and were sinking into a collection of chairs and couches. All were zombies to the Ecstasy and their senses were overpowered by the euphoria of little more than a breeze.

As Ravi attempted to navigate through the undulating bodies, a young woman grabbed him with both hands.

"You're electric...I can barely hold onto you." Her head drifted on her neck and her body swayed back and forth like seaweed in a changing tide. "Touch me, but don't kiss me. I wouldn't be able to take it." Ravi reached out and gently touched her arm. She jerked her body up against his before quickly falling away again. "Can you feel that connection?" She brushed her lower body against his, let out an orgasmic moan, and fell against him. "I can hardly stand to be this close to you. You're so powerful."

Ravi looked almost longingly at her as she smiled, disengaged, and disappeared back into the crowd. This was nothing more than moments of happiness in a dark tunnel, and for the first time, he could not imagine why anyone would want for more. He could no longer understand what validation he had been searching for in his books and studies. He could no longer justify his quest for truth when life was nothing more than random connections like those in this rotting tunnel.

He watched this collection of human kelp drift aimlessly in front of him until the pain in his ankle was no longer dulled by the scent of body odor, smoke and sewage. As he turned to go, the young woman appeared in front of him again. She grabbed him by the ears and locked her lips to his. Her whole body shook, her lips quivered, and her throat buzzed as she fought to stay engaged. When she finally released him, she said, "I can't imagine a greater thrill than that."

Ravi continued into the darkness fighting tears of pain and regret with every step. He kept one hand on the wall as he followed the noise of the road above to guide him. Ahead of him was Gibson Street, and just beyond it was his chance to exit into Kelvingrove Park. The rays of light filtering down from the street lights above provided an extra spring in his step, and he pulled himself up the unlocked gate. He slowly pushed it open, and limped cautiously out into the night.

"Ravi." Sophia was sitting on the bench in front of him with legs crossed and arms folded around her. He started to limp towards her, and she sprang up to help him the rest of the way to the bench. He winced as he sat in a heap of dirt, sweat, pain and fear.

"I'm sorry," she muttered softly, looking at the University on the hill.

"For what?"

"Everything. This is not how our life should have been."

"What were you expecting?"

"I'm pretty sure that I was expecting the same as you. I was expecting that we would be living in a sandstone walkup, we would be spending our days researching the mysteries of the world, and we would be coming home each night tackling the mysteries of children." She turned to look at him in a way she had not done for years. "That is what was supposed to happen to us."

"Are we really too late for that?"

She looked back into the darkness, pondering her response as she slowly nodded her head. "There are many things that we can't ever control. There are many things that become uncontrollable. And then there are those things in this world someone else takes control of for you. I am afraid this is a moment in the last category."

"What are you saying?"

"I love you Ravi. I always have, and I always will." Her eyes began to fill with tears until she couldn't look at him anymore. "But the world is bigger than both of us, and saving it requires some sacrifices."

She wiped the tears from her eyes, gave one sniffle, and stood up. Her tears suddenly dissipated as she spoke with dry resolve. "I am truly sorry that, in this case, I had to sacrifice you."

As Ravi stared at her, mouth agape and eyebrows curled, a white van roared through the gates with the door open before screeching to a halt right next to them. Sophia stood aside as three men jumped out and drug Ravi to his feet. The indifferent look on Sophia's face was the last thing Ravi saw as the hood came down over his head and a zip tie anchored it to his neck.

Chapter 8

Ravi's arms were chained under his legs. Music in the distance was continually thumping in an unfamiliar pattern that seemed to have no beginning or end. His whole body swung through sensations, as if it was being crushed at one moment and in free fall the next. He couldn't tell if he was upright, lying on his side, or even hanging upside down, suspended from his toes. He could only smell a mixture of his own sweat and the stale, black fabric over his head. He couldn't tell for certain if his eyes were open or shut.

He was kicked and punched at random times. Sometimes he would only feel the residual pain and other times the whole kick, which made it impossible for him to tell if he was asleep or awake during the beatings.

In the blackness, he struggled to find the surface of his skin. He was sure that he must be able to sense where his skin ended and his clothes began, so he set out to try and find every twist and turn of his body. At one point he thought that he had felt the tips of his fingers, so he tried to work back along the surface of his hand. But just as he thought he had found the root of a hair on the back of his hand, the dull pain of a kick or strike made him realize that he had actually been asleep and had not moved at all.

Before he could succeed in finding his ends, he was pulled by his armpits until he landed in what he was certain was an upright position. His hands were momentarily released and he felt his arms move as they were chained again behind him.

The thumping music stopped. Someone removed the hood from his head and he struggled to blink back the bright light of the room. Once his irises had contracted to the point where his eyelids were again able to darken his vision, he tried to look around the room. Like a young baby, he attempted to peek out through mostly closed eyelids, hoping to recognize something familiar.

The room looked like a concrete box, and he was sitting by a hard, maybe steel, table. Across the table was an orange object.

"I told you. Guys like me, we're all the same. We don't think it will happen to us."

"Angus?"

"Yup. Guess the earth moved on us." Ravi was finally able to open his eyes wide enough to make out Angus' bloody face across the room. One of his eyes was completely swelled shut. The other side of his face was blotched with blood where it had been running down to his neck. When he saw that Ravi was finally able to see him, he was quick with a grin. "If you think I'm looking bad, you should see the other guy. I think he stubbed his toe on my face." As disoriented and broken as he was, Ravi smiled.

"There you go. You'll find humanity again," Angus said.

The large steel door opened in the middle of the room, and a man in a grey suit walked in. He sat down at the table with Ravi and Angus and clasped his hands on the table in front of him.

"I apologize for your current predicament," he began in a heavy Italian accent, "but I can assure you that you can both return to your lives as if nothing has happened if you help me verify what I need to know."

"Nope," replied Angus. "That won't be happening."

"I beg your pardon?"

"Nope. Our lives will not go back to normal, and you will not get what you need."

The man was visibly disturbed by Angus' immediate and hostile response. "What makes you say that? I can most definitely make this all go away for you."

"Nope. You're not the man in charge." Angus' sneer turned into a full smile as the man squirmed in his seat.

"I most definitely am the man in charge. I can get you whatever you need. I can set you free."

"Repeating a lie just means I have to hear it twice. You will get nothing." The man turned to address Ravi, but before he could speak, Angus broke in again. "Ravi, I'm sure your brain is a little rattled right now, but don't say a word to this guy. If you talk to him, they kill you. If you don't, he's a goner."

The man's face went white as he sat back in his chair and looked from Ravi to Angus and back again. "I just need your help—"

"Well you should have thought of that before we ended up here you little cunt!" Angus screamed. "Gabriele, Ratzinger is going to string you up by your ears and your toes and tear every piece of your body apart in thimble sized chunks! I would rather be me than you right now!"

The man, who Angus identified as Gabriele, was visibly shaken. His feet were shifting on the cement floor, his right leg was bouncing, and his head was shaking from side to side. "This is not how this is supposed to go..."

"You're telling me this is not how this is supposed to go? Grow some bullocks you silly cunt! Me being here is definitely not how this is supposed to go! You stealing Church secrets is not how this is supposed to go!" Angus violently hurled his words at Gabriele, and his chair jumped along the floor with every word.

"I would happily be slowly dismembered over the course of thirty days if I was offered just two hours of time with you and a pocket knife! Get the fuck out of here and bring back Muller...I'm embarrassed to have to even see you, you little grease stain!" Angus spat, and Gabriele jumped backwards out of his chair.

Gabriele paced the floor for a few moments as he bit at his fingers. Ravi struggled to make sense of it all. "Ravi, I just need you to—"

Before he could finish, Angus was back on the attack. "Get the fuck out of here you silly fucking cunt! You put us here! We will not help you! I would rather see myself bound by my small intestines that give you any chance of living even one more day without fear! Get the fuck out of our sight, and bring back Muller!"

Gabriele looked as if he was about to cry. He stood there biting his finger and he looked pleadingly at Ravi. "Please..."

Ravi sat looking up at him. His head was clearing and his courage was building.

"No," he said, quietly and firmly.

Gabriele covered his eyes and began to shudder. Ravi looked at Angus who had a wide smile on his face. "These are the moments to live for, Ravi," Angus said. "This is true freedom."

"That's enough!" The steel door again swung open, and a large, academic looking German man entered the room, followed by three darkly dressed men. He was dressed in the black cassock of a Catholic cardinal, and he took his hat off as he approached Gabriele. He came nose to nose with Gabriele, and Ravi could see his seething anger spilling out from between his clenched teeth. He backhanded Gabriele with one swift, full-arm swing and struck him to the ground. "Get out of my sight."

As Gabriele slinked to the corner of the room behind Ravi, the Cardinal addressed Angus. "Very clever. Congratulations to you on making that vermin cry. Now, good night." Before Angus could say anything, one of the men had thrown his chair backwards and the other kicked his head as it fell. Ravi could hear the snapping of bones as Angus's forearms, which were chained behind the chair back, were crushed against the floor. The two men who entered with the Cardinal disconnected Angus from the chair, dragged him across the floor, and hoisted him up by the feet until he was suspended from the ceiling. Angus's body swayed lifelessly from side to side. Then the Cardinal turned to Ravi.

"I have been reading about your exploits and am shocked that at nearly every turn you continued to be an unwitting passenger in the events unfolding around you." He pulled the chair in front of Ravi and sat down facing him. "For example, do you even know who I am?"

Ravi slowly shook his head.

"I am Archbishop Gerhard Ludwig Muller, Prefect of the Congregation for the Doctrine of the Faith. Do you know what that means?"

Ravi again slowly shook his head.

"I would suppose that this is precisely my problem with this situation," he sighed as he leaned back in the chair. "You are dangerous because you didn't even know you needed to pick a side. You have been played by everyone, and have no idea what to protect and what to share. That makes you a real threat."

With a wave of his finger, another man positioned himself behind Ravi.

"What side should I be on?" asked Ravi.

"At this point? God's."

With a quick biting sensation on the side of his neck, Ravi's world was again plunged into darkness.

***

In his blackness, Ravi heard the door open. A group of people had entered the room. One stepped with purpose while the rest scampered to keep up. The leader barked in Italian: not the melodic Italian used by heroes in movies, or the Italian dialect from the streets of Italy. This was the throaty, broken Italian of a foreigner. The rage in his voice was clear, and the multi-language responses were laden with fear.

"How did you let this one live this long? What is he doing still hanging here? This one is about six months past his expiration date. Is this you? Are you responsible for him being here?"

"I wouldn't say that it's...Uh...I wouldn't exactly—"

"You wouldn't say? You wouldn't say?! That is exactly the reason I needed to come here and clean this shit up. What the fuck am I here for? How is it possible none of you sorted any of your own shit out? Give me a fucking gun."

Everyone shuffled across the room behind the large, enraged leader. Ravi heard a metallic click followed by a clack, and Angus started to whimper. One set of leather souls shuffled on the floor like brushes on a snare drum.

"Now you fucking whimper?" the gunman said, kneeling below Angus's head. "How long have you known this was coming? You boasted about this already. What did you say to that sorry piece of shit over there? You all think you're different? Where are your balls now?"

There was more shuffling.

"Fucking Christ! This is why you don't hang a man upside down like this! When he pisses himself it gets all over you! Look at this you fucking fools. Is this your first time? Am I working with a bunch of virgins here?"

The rope creaked, and Angus gave an audible cry.

"I'm pulling your hair, not your fingernails! Shut the fuck up!"

When Angus could only muffle his crying, Ravi heard the sound of the end of the gun striking flesh.

"If they don't shut the fuck up, you plug the hole. For fuck sake, you act like you've never seen this."

Angus's crying was again muffled, as if something had been jammed in his mouth.

"Anyone want to give last rights? No one? All right then," the gunman said. "Any sins to confess? Is that a no, or has the gun got your tongue? No matter, thanks for your confession, your sins are absolved, see you in heaven."

Ravi knew for certain that he was awake. The sound of the muffled gun made him jump. In the momentarily silent room, his heart began to race to the rhythmic sound of a swinging flesh pendulum on the end of a rope.

"Give me a fucking towel so I can clean this shit off of my hands. Well then, come here and I'll use your fucking clothes!"

Ravi turned away from Angus' dripping corpse to see the gunman using the red lining of a cardinal's robe to clean the gun he held. When the gunman finally turned to look at him, Ravi recognized him in an instant.

"I assume English is best for you?" Pope Benedict waited for a moment, clearly irritated by any delay, and went on. "Although I assume you got the gist of that, regardless of the language?"

With his hand mostly clean, he threw the robe he was using down and approached Ravi.

"Now I know you'll probably blame me for the mess you're in right now, although you'll only have a few more moments for that, so I figured I'd reintroduce you to the nitwit who caused all of this."

He motioned over his shoulder to Gabriele who stood in the middle of the followers. "Gabriele decided to be double-oh-seven for the past few years and needed someone to do what he was too cowardly to do. Your brother's blood, that pile-of-shit's blood, your blood: it's all on his head. Gabriele, come say hello." When Gabriele wouldn't move, Benedict started to walk towards him. "Get over here now, and tell this man how sorry you are for killing him," Benedict growled, grabbing Gabriele by the front of his shirt.

Gabriele crumpled and hung from Benedict's hand. A Cardinal reached down and helped drag the now sobbing man forward.

"You fucking did this, and you will be the one who lives. Why are you crying, you coward? You nearly bring down this Church, and you are crying? If there were a god, he would have been proud to sleep in before creating an embarrassment like you. Get to your fucking feet!"

Benedict pulled Gabriele to his feet as he wept. Ravi tried to blink back the tears that were now filling his eyes. He could see Angus swinging like a hunk of meet in the background. He could feel his body starting to shake, and he began whimpering uncontrollable.

"Look at what you are doing to him?" Benedict said, turning to Ravi. "Was your life really such a waste that you deserved this? Do you deserve to be in the middle of this? Did you ask for this?"

With each question his voice became shriller, the anger poured more freely, and Ravi began to cry more violently. "No..." was all he could force out between sobs.

"You could be having beers right now, maybe even making love with that beautiful young lady. But where are you?" Ravi's head fell. He could no longer see through his tears. "You are here because this piece of filth used you to get to me. To my Church: To my world!"

He dragged Gabriele forward until he was just inches from Ravi's face. "Look at what you have done! Look him in the eyes you piece of filth!" He yanked Ravi's head up by his hair. Benedict's fingers ripped at his scalp like it was a beheaded trophy. As the tears flowed from his eyes and his chest heaved, Ravi could see Benedict's hand cradled around Gabriele's which now held the bloody gun. The metal was still warm as they pressed it against Ravi's brow. Ravi's vision faded through the tears and the noise vanished.

Like the moment in the Tap when the blast killed his brother, this flash had nearly disappeared before the force hit him. His world faded from a flash of white to an afterlife of blackness.

Epilogue

On February 28, 2013, Pope Benedict XVI became only the ninth Roman Catholic Pope to ever resign: a move so rare it had not happened for over 600 years. In the ensuing fight to lead the Church, many sins were revealed, and only those who took part in these battles for the Church's future can truly predict the impact of elevating Cardinal Bergoglio to Pope Francis.

In the centuries to come, future generations may learn what loose ends Pope Benedict XVI may have tied up and which sins may remain unpunished.

www.ingramcontent.com/pod-product-compliance
Lightning Source LLC
Chambersburg PA
CBHW060354180626
46817CB00008B/3007